PAUL ROBESON

Other titles in the *African-American Biography Library*

BOOKER T. WASHINGTON
"Character Is Power"
ISBN-13: 978-0-7660-2535-6
ISBN-10:   0-7660-2535-7

COLIN POWELL
"Have a Vision. Be Demanding"
ISBN-13: 978-0-7660-2464-9
ISBN-10:   0-7660-2464-4

DUKE ELLINGTON
"I Live With Music"
ISBN-13: 978-0-7660-2702-2
ISBN-10:   0-7660-2702-3

GWENDOLYN BROOKS
"Poetry Is Life Distilled"
ISBN-13: 978-0-7660-2292-8
ISBN-10:   0-7660-2292-7

HALLE BERRY
"Beauty Is Not Just Physical"
ISBN-13: 978-0-7660-2467-0
ISBN-10:   0-7660-2467-9

JACKIE ROBINSON
"All I Ask Is That You Respect Me as a Human Being"
ISBN-13: 978-0-7660-2461-8
ISBN-10:   0-7660-2461-X

LANGSTON HUGHES
"Life Makes Poems"
ISBN-13: 978-0-7660-2468-7
ISBN-10:   0-7660-2468-7

LOUIS ARMSTRONG
"Jazz Is Played From The Heart"
ISBN-13: 978-0-7660-2700-8
ISBN-10:   0-7660-2700-7

MARTIN LUTHER KING, JR.
"We Shall Overcome"
ISBN-13: 978-0-7660-1774-0
ISBN-10:   0-7660-1774-5

MAYA ANGELOU
"Diversity Makes For a Rich Tapestry"
ISBN-13: 978-0-7660-2469-4
ISBN-10:   0-7660-2469-5

MUHAMMAD ALI
"I Am the Greatest"
ISBN-13: 978-0-7660-2460-1
ISBN-10:   0-7660-2460-1

OPRAH WINFREY
"I Don't Believe in Failure"
ISBN-13: 978-0-7660-2462-5
ISBN-10:   0-7660-2462-8

RAY CHARLES
"I Got Music Inside Me"
ISBN-13: 978-0-7660-2701-5
ISBN-10:   0-7660-2701-5

ROSA PARKS
"Tired of Giving In"
ISBN-13:   978-0-7660-2463-2
ISBN-10: 0-7660-2463-6

WILL SMITH
"I Like Blending a Message With Comedy"
ISBN-13: 978-0-7660-2465-6
ISBN-10:   0-7660-2465-2

ZORA NEALE HURSTON
"I Have Been In Sorrow's Kitchen"
ISBN-13: 978-0-7660-2536-3
ISBN-10:   0-7660-2536-5

AFRICAN-AMERICAN BIOGRAPHY LIBRARY

PAUL ROBESON

"I Want To Make Freedom Ring"

Carin T. Ford

Series Consultant:
Dr. Russell L. Adams, Chairman
Department of
Afro-American Studies,
Howard University

Enslow Publishers, Inc.
40 Industrial Road
Box 398
Berkeley Heights, NJ 07922
USA

http://www.enslow.com

"I WANT TO MAKE FREEDOM RING."
—Paul Robeson

Acknowledgments

Thank you to Director of Education and Web Development Amanda V. Casabianca and Director of Research and Archives Bonnie Weiss of the Bay Area Paul Robeson Centennial Committee for their work as advisors.

Also, a special gratitude goes to Paul Robeson, Jr., for providing many of the photos in this book through the Paul Robeson Foundation.

Copyright © 2008 by Carin T. Ford

All rights reserved.

No part of this book may be reproduced by any means without the written permission of the publisher.

Library of Congress Cataloging-in-Publication Data

Ford, Carin T.
    Paul Robeson : "I want to make freedom ring" / Carin T. Ford.
      p. cm. — (African-American biography library)
    Includes bibliographical references and index.
    ISBN-13: 978-0-7660-2703-9
    ISBN-10: 0-7660-2703-1
    1. Robeson, Paul, 1898-1976—Juvenile literature. 2. African Americans—Biography—Juvenile literature. 3. Actors—United States—Biography—Juvenile literature.
4. Singers—United States—Biography—Juvenile literature. 5. Political activists—United States—Biography—Juvenile literature. I. Title.
    E185.97.R63F67 2008
    782.0092—dc22
    [B]
                                                  2006038000

Printed in the United States of America

10 9 8 7 6 5 4 3 2 1

To Our Readers:
We have done our best to make sure all Internet Addresses in this book were active and appropriate when we went to press. However, the author and the publisher have no control over and assume no liability for the material available on those Internet sites or on other Web sites they may link to. Any comments or suggestions can be sent by e-mail to comments@enslow.com or to the address on the back cover.

Every effort has been made to locate all copyright holders of material used in this book. If any errors or omissions have occurred, corrections will be made in future editions of this book.

Illustration Credits: AndrewBurgin.Com, p. 94; Enslow Publishers, Inc., p. 11; NYPL, Astar, Lenox and Tilden Foundations, p. 42; The Paul Robeson Foundation., pp. 5, 7, 10, 22, 30, 37, 40, 48, 53, 55, 58, 60, 63, 66, 69, 70, 72, 79, 81, 86, 90, 102, 107, 112; © Roy Mullis, Shutterstock.com, p. 76; Rutgers Special Collections, pp. 23, 26, 46, 49; The Library of Congress, pp. 6, 98; Tim Larsen/Associated Press, p. 114; Westfield Historical Society, pp. 15, 20.

Cover Illustrations: The Library of Congress (top); The Paul Robeson Foundation (bottom).

Contents

1. Rising to the Top 7
2. Years of Hardship 10
3. College and Career Choices 22
4. On Stage 37
5. Beyond the United States 48
6. The Spell of the Soviet Union 58
7. Political Interests 70
8. Under Suspicion 81
9. In the Thick of It 90
10. A Career Halted 102

    Chronology 116
    Chapter Notes 118
    Further Reading 124
    Internet Addresses 125
    Index 126

Paul Robeson

Chapter 1

Rising to the Top

When seventeen-year-old Paul Robeson entered Rutgers College as a freshman, only two other African-American students had ever attended the school. The year was 1915, and Robeson was the only African American out of a class of five hundred. It was not an easy role for him, yet Robeson would always act in a way that reflected well on all black Americans. Life at college would definitely test his resolve.

Robeson was an outstanding athlete and he decided to try out for the football team. His father encouraged him while at the same time reminding his son that he was attending college to get a good education; sports came second.

Robeson was tall and had a sturdy build. His height of six foot two inches was several inches taller than the average

PAUL ROBESON

player on the Rutgers team and at 190 pounds, he was at least 20 pounds heavier. His height, weight, and natural athletic ability made Robeson an excellent candidate for making the team.

But there had never been a black athlete on Rutgers' football team before. Most of the players did not want Robeson there, and they did their best to keep him from joining the squad. They ganged up on Robeson during practice; several players would jump on him in a tackle or Robeson would find his movements blocked by two players at once. Because football equipment was not the same in the early 1900s as it is today, Robeson wore only a small amount of padding in his shirt and pants and a thin leather helmet. On his first day of practice, his nose was broken, his right shoulder was sprained, and there were bruises all over his body. Robeson was so severely injured that he had to remain in bed for ten days in order to recover.

> On his first day of practice, his nose was broken, his right shoulder was sprained, and there were bruises all over his body.

Robeson was not sure he could handle this kind of treatment—he was not even sure he wanted to. Yet he had been raised to respect himself and respect his race. He needed to do what was right.

"If you want to quit school go ahead," said his brother, Ben, "but I wouldn't like to think and our father wouldn't like to think that our family had a quitter in it."[1]

RISING TO THE TOP

At the next practice, the team members once again hurt Paul Robeson. When he was lying on the ground after being tackled, a player purposely stomped on his hand. Although no bones were broken, Robeson suddenly became furious. He grabbed his attacker on the next play and raised him high over his head, wanting to smash him to the ground. Yet before he could do that, Coach G. Foster Sanford stopped him. He told Robeson he had made the varsity team. He also told the other players if anyone ever purposely hurt Robeson again, they would be cut from the squad.

Even as a freshman, Robeson was one of the starting players on the squad. He would eventually become the star of the team and be voted onto the All-American football team in 1917 and 1918.

Paul Robeson would face many obstacles in his life, but he would always stand up for himself and what he believed was right.

He was *not* a quitter.

Chapter 2

Years of Hardship

Paul Leroy Robeson was born April 9, 1898, in Princeton, New Jersey. His parents were William Drew Robeson and Maria Louisa Bustill. Paul's parents were not young when he was born. William was fifty-three and Maria was forty-five. Paul was the youngest of five surviving children: William Drew, Jr.; Marian; Benjamin; and Reeve. Paul would grow up to become a man who stood up for his beliefs. This was a quality he inherited from his parents, especially his father.

Paul's father had been born a slave. In 1860, fifteen-year-old William escaped from the North Carolina plantation where he worked. He was able to make his way North with the help of the Underground Railroad. This was not actually a railroad but a network of secret routes

YEARS OF HARDSHIP

NEW JERSEY

Paul Robeson spent most of his life in New Jersey and New York.

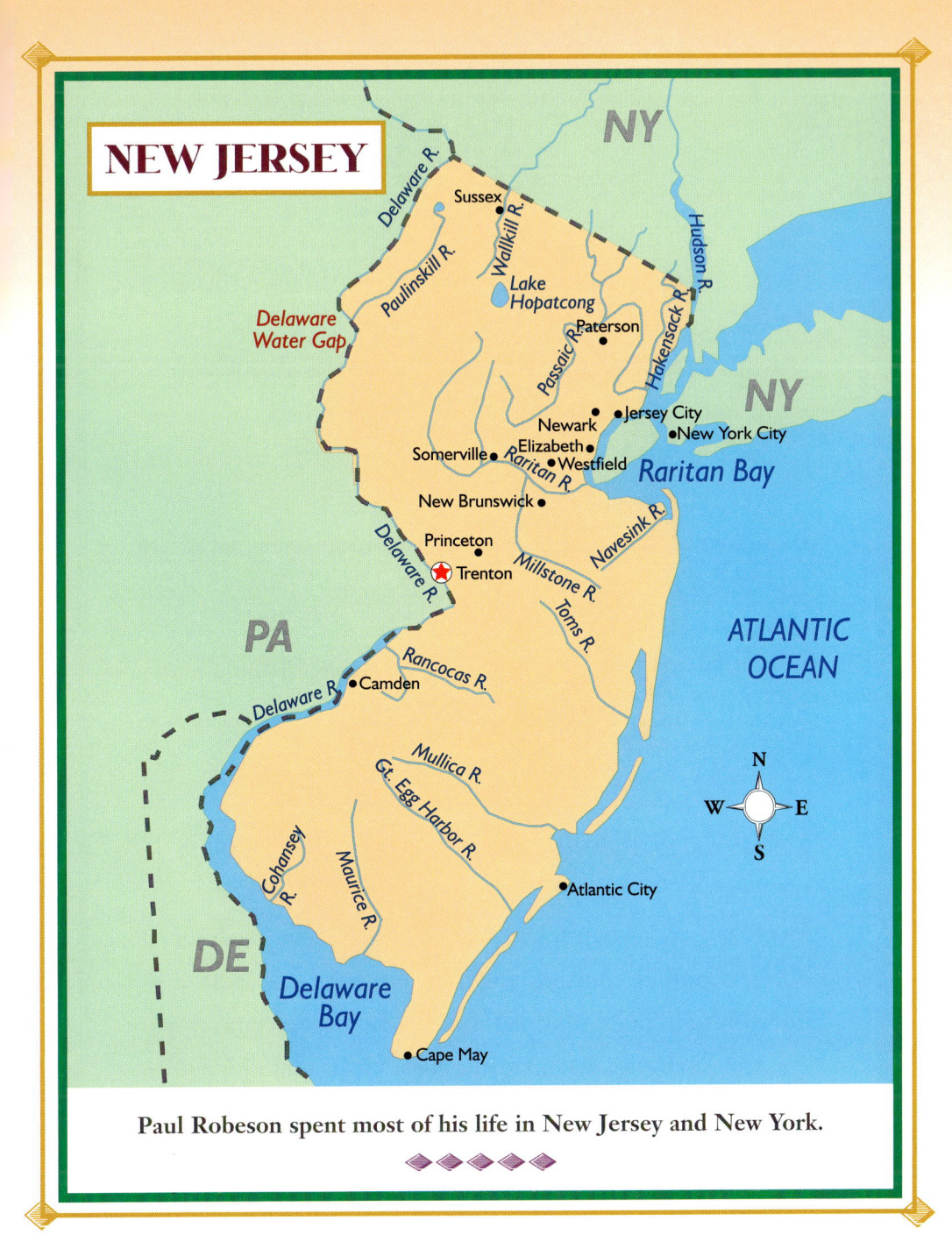

used by slaves in the 1800s to escape to the free states in the North or Canada. William took the last name Robeson, which he based on the plantation owner's last name of Roberson.

The Civil War had begun in 1861, and William became one of more than two hundred thousand African Americans to fight for the Union. He joined the Union army in Pennsylvania and worked on construction.

When the war ended, William studied hard and received a basic education. Earning money as a farmworker, he enrolled in Lincoln University and earned a Bachelor of Arts degree in 1873. Three years later, he received a degree in sacred theology, which focused on religious beliefs and practices.

While he was attending the university, William met Maria Bustill, his future wife. Her family background was a mixture of African American, Delaware Indian, and English Quaker. One of her relations worked on the Underground Railroad helping slaves reach freedom in the North. Maria believed in the value of education as much as her husband; she was a schoolteacher and aided her husband in putting together his sermons. She also joined him in helping care for members of the community.

After working for a short time as a pastor in Wilkes-Barre, Pennsylvania, William Robeson took the position of minister at the Witherspoon Street Presbyterian Church in Princeton, New Jersey.

YEARS OF HARDSHIP

Paul had many relatives living nearby, including several from his father's side who had left North Carolina, anxious to get away from the South. As head of the African-American church, Paul's father held an important position in the community. He was known as a man who would fight for the rights of African Americans and as someone with strong moral values.

Despite this position, William was accused of not handling the church's business matters well and was asked to leave. William had been a minister at the church for twenty years, and many members of his congregation did not want him to leave; they stood behind him. When he delivered his farewell sermon, the crowd was so large there was not enough room for everyone to sit down.

The family remained in Princeton, although a far worse tragedy was in store for them. One winter's day in 1904, when Paul was only five years old, his mother was cleaning the living room. A stove filled with hot coals sat in the living room. When Maria tried to move the stove to

Princeton

Although nearly 20 percent of the residents who lived in Princeton were African American, the town was heavily segregated in the early 1900s. Black children had to attend different schools than whites—a high-school education was not available to them in Princeton. Families such as the Robesons had to send their children to schools in other towns if they were to continue with their studies.

clean behind it, a piece of coal suddenly fell on her dress. The dress caught fire and she was badly burned. Maria was in terrible pain, and after several days she died.

Paul did not remember much of his mother since he was so young when she died. He now lived with his father and brother Ben and the three of them struggled to survive. His older siblings had moved away from home by this time; his sister, Marian, went to school in North Carolina.

William Robeson was without a job and without a wife. He found work as a coachman, driving Princeton students. He also hauled ashes with a horse and wagon. Yet he did not complain or show any bitterness. Paul would always remember his father as a man filled with dignity.

Alone with his father, Paul spent his days with books. William Robeson made sure his son's time was not wasted.

"If I had had some time . . . that wasn't blocked out and filled in for me, I think my imagination would have been more developed," Paul said. "As it is I've almost none. All my time was crowded with lessons to learn, games to play, books to read. I never can remember having had hours in which I had nothing to do, and had actually to entertain myself out of my own mind."[1]

Three years after his mother's death, Paul moved with his brother and father to Westfield, New Jersey. There, William Robeson ran a grocery store. He lived with his sons in the store's attic. He did any washing and cooking in a small shack that was attached to the building.

YEARS OF HARDSHIP

St. Luke A.M.E. Zion Church was built by Paul Robeson's father.

Yet William Robeson was anxious to be connected with a church, and he soon started the Downer Street St. Luke A.M.E. Zion Church. This was an African Methodist Episcopal church and the members were black men and women who had once lived in the South.

The women of the church took the Robesons under their wing, making sure the boys had enough to eat and that someone was available to watch young Paul when his father was called away.

Paul also was mothered by relatives and friends who lived nearby. If he ever wanted to eat dinner or spend the night away from home, aunts, uncles, cousins, and neighbors opened their homes to him. "You'll grow up to be a credit to us, you'll see," they said.[2] It seemed as if nearly everyone who came in contact with Paul thought he would do something great when he grew up.

"There must have been moments when I felt the sorrows

of a motherless child, but what I most remember from my youngest days was an abiding sense of comfort and security," said Paul Robeson later.[3] The Robesons' friends and neighbors in Westfield said Paul was a nice boy with a kind heart.

"I didn't know what I was supposed to be when I grew up," Paul said. "A minister like my father? A teacher like my mother? But whatever the vocation might be, I must grow up to be a 'credit to the race,'" as they said.[4]

By the time Paul was eleven, his father had become involved with the St. Thomas A.M.E. Zion church in Somerville, New Jersey. Father and son were on their own because Ben had left home to attend Biddle University in North Carolina. Like his father, Ben would go on to become pastor of a church.

Paul and his father were very close. They played checkers together, and William Robeson often gave his son a speech to memorize. William was a wonderful speaker with a deep, rich voice and he encouraged his son to develop a talent for giving speeches. He carefully went over the words with Paul and taught him how to use his voice to his best advantage. Most important, he told Paul that he should always try to help people who were not treated fairly.

Paul admired his father a great deal. "He had the greatest speaking voice I have ever heard," he said. "How proudly,

YEARS OF HARDSHIP

as a boy, I walked at his side, my hand in his, as he moved among the people!"[5]

There was one time, however, that Paul did not listen to his father. When he was about ten years old, Paul ran away from his father when he was asked to do something. His father called to him, but Paul kept running. As Paul raced across the street, his father hurried after him and suddenly tripped and fell.

"I was horrified. I hurried back, helped Pop to his feet. He had knocked out one of his teeth," said Paul. "I have never forgotten the emotions—the sense of horror, shame, ingratitude, selfishness—that overwhelmed me. I adored him . . . and here I had hurt him, disobeyed him!"[6] It was the last time Paul would disobey his father.

William Robeson was a strict father and he was concerned about setting the right example for Paul. Throughout his boyhood, Paul had many responsibilities. He helped with chores, took on outside jobs to pay for school expenses, participated in church activities, and was also expected to maintain top grades in school. When Paul was twelve, he had a job working in a kitchen. He worked on a farm two years later and after that was hired in brickyards and shipyards. By the time he was in his late teens, Paul had a job as a waiter at a hotel in Rhode Island during the summer.

Paul did all that his father asked—and more. In Somerville, New Jersey, he attended James J. Jamison's

PAUL ROBESON

> The more Paul achieved at school in sports and music, the more Principal Ackerman disliked him.

school for African-American students. Here he earned excellent grades and was popular with the other students. After graduating from the Jamison School, Paul then went to an integrated school, where black and white students attended classes together. The Washington School went up to the seventh grade and Paul graduated at the top of the class. He spent eighth grade at a school for African Americans in Somerville and then began attending Somerville High School.

The high school enrolled about two hundred students. Of these, fewer than twelve were African Americans. White classmates treated Robeson and the other black students fairly and Paul had many friends.

Yet the school's principal, Dr. Ackerman, was known by many of the students—even the white students—as a prejudiced man. The more Paul achieved at school in sports and music, the more Principal Ackerman disliked him.

One day, he sent Paul home because he was late. Paul's father began to scold Paul. But Paul said to him, "Listen, Pop, I'm bigger now. I don't care what *you* do to me, but if that hateful old principal ever lays a hand on me, I swear I'll try my best to break his neck."[7]

YEARS OF HARDSHIP

In spite of Ackerman, Paul was respected for his talent in sports, debating, academics, and singing. Paul joined the glee club—although Ackerman did not want him as a soloist. But Paul had known he had talent since the day he first sang with his brothers Bill and Ben.

"We started off with gusto . . . Paul was bearing down . . . with boyish glee; in fact, all of us were," said Ben. "Out of all the discord, Bill yelled: 'Wait a minute, hit that note again, Paul.' Paul hit out of the lot, and Bill said, 'Paul, you can sing.'"[8]

Paul took part in the school's production of *Shakespeare at the Water Cure* in 1915. It featured characters from Shakespeare's plays such as *Romeo and Juliet*, *Hamlet*, and *Othello* in a modern setting for that time. Paul had a singing role in the play and when one of his teachers heard his deep bass voice, she told him to join the school's chorus.

Although prejudice was not prevalent at his high school, Paul did not feel comfortable attending school parties and dances because of the color of his skin.

"There was always the feeling that—well, something unpleasant might happen," he said.[9]

He sometimes worried that the white students would resent his success in so many areas. Although he was very modest, it was hard to hide his achievements, especially in sports where Paul seemed to perform equally well in basketball, track, tennis, and football. In one football game, the rough players of Phillipsburg High School focused on

PAUL ROBESON

Paul Robeson, front, poses with this Westfield, New Jersey, baseball team.

Paul as the player to stop. Although the heavyset boys tackled him and piled on him, Paul still was able to score a touchdown.

When Paul was a senior, he competed in a statewide public-speaking contest. Paul was up against five or six other boys, all of whom were white. The other boys went first, and although they spoke well, no one speech was obviously better than another. Paul's turn was last and he

YEARS OF HARDSHIP

spoke about Toussaint L'Ouverture, a black revolutionary from Haiti. Paul's speech—with its unusual subject matter and his powerful delivery—was outstanding. He wound up winning third place.

Paul also participated that year in a statewide exam for a four-year scholarship to Rutgers College (today known as Rutgers University). Paul's family and several teachers tried to urge him to attend a smaller, all-black school, but Paul was determined to go to a large school. "Here was a decisive point in my life," he said. "Deep in my heart from that day on was a conviction which none of the Ackermans of America would ever be able to shake. Equality might be denied, but I knew I was not inferior."[10]

One huge obstacle was the exam itself. Most of the other students had already taken an exam months earlier that covered the first three years of their high school curriculum. They now only needed to take this second exam, which covered their fourth year of school.

Paul, however, did not find out about the scholarship exam in time. He had to take the entire test in one sitting, covering all four years of high school academics. Although he had very little time to prepare, Paul took the exam and won the scholarship. He would attend Rutgers.

Chapter 3

College and Career Choices

At Rutgers College, athletics played a big part in Paul Robeson's life. Once he made a place for himself on the varsity football team, the next step was facing prejudice from other colleges.

There were some tense experiences—especially when Rutgers was playing against teams from the South. Georgia Tech and William and Mary College in Virginia would not even compete against a college with African-American players. When Rutgers was scheduled to play against Washington and Lee University, also located in Virginia, they had to pull Robeson from the lineup in order to hold the game. Some of the Rutgers players were angry at this, and Robeson himself considered quitting the team and possibly transferring to a different college.

COLLEGE AND CAREER CHOICES

But he stayed at Rutgers, and when the school was scheduled to play a game against West Virginia, that school's coach demanded that Robeson be removed from the competition. This time, however, the Rutgers coach would not agree to take Robeson out of the lineup.

When the two teams faced each other at the start of the game, the player standing across from Robeson told him that if Robeson tried to touch him, he would cut out

Robeson was the only black player on an otherwise all-white Rutgers football team.

PAUL ROBESON

Robeson's heart. At the sound of the whistle, Robeson headed straight for the player, knocking into him with brutal force. "I touched you that time," he said. "How did you like it?"[1]

The final score of the game was a tie, and when the teams lined up to shake hands at the end of the game, every West Virginia player shook Robeson's hand.

Just as he had been in high school, Robeson was outstanding in many areas in college. Besides sports, where he starred on football, basketball, and baseball teams as well as track and field, he showed tremendous talent in debating and singing in the glee club. For four years in a row, Robeson won the class prize for public speaking.

Robeson had a huge, deep singing voice in the bass-baritone range and was a more than welcome addition to the glee club. Yet because of his skin color, he only sang with the chorus during concerts held at Rutgers. When the glee club traveled to perform at other locations, Robeson was not included.

Robeson learned to deal with this treatment. He tolerated it because performing in the glee club brought him money, which he badly needed. Every time he sang at a home concert, people remarked on Robeson's outstanding singing ability. As a result, he was often hired to perform at private concerts.

At these private jobs, he would sing several songs as well as give a speech—which he did equally well—and

COLLEGE AND CAREER CHOICES

then sing some more. For his efforts, he was paid about fifty dollars. To earn more money, Robeson also worked in New York's Grand Central Station carrying people's suitcases.

During Robeson's junior year, his father died suddenly at the age of seventy-three. Three days later, Robeson competed in a public speaking contest, something he had promised his father he would do. Robeson's speech was, in effect, a memorial to his father. He spoke of the lack of decent educational opportunities for African Americans

Prejudice at College

Throughout his years in college, Robeson frequently was forced to deal with being treated as less than a full member of a specific club or group. Although he was voted into the college's literary society, he was not allowed to take part in the festivities when members were inducted. The new members also bought treats at an ice cream and candy store—but the store's owner would not serve an African American.

When Robeson reluctantly agreed to attend a college dance, he purposely kept away from the dancers and, instead, stood on the balcony occasionally singing to the students below. Although Robeson was hurt deeply by these events, he did not let anyone else know how he really felt.

and the unfair treatment of black people in general. He won the contest.

Robeson continued with these thoughts when it came time to write his senior paper. He wrote about the Fourteenth Amendment, which gave African Americans full legal rights as U.S. citizens. In his speech, Robeson focused on the hope that one day black people would be looked upon as equal to whites.

When Paul Robeson graduated from Rutgers in 1919, his top grades won him the honor of being first in the class. He was also one of four students out of eighty asked to join the Cap and Skull honor society. This was the oldest honor society at Rutgers College, and it admitted students based on excellence in academics,

Robeson was valedictorian of his class when he graduated from Rutgers.

COLLEGE AND CAREER CHOICES

athletics, the arts, and public service. He was also a member of Phi Beta Kappa, another honor society.

Robeson's valedictory speech at graduation centered on how important it was for African Americans to help themselves in order to improve their position in the world. He also talked of his hopes that one day "black and white shall clasp friendly hands."[2] When he finished, the crowd cheered and applauded.

While at Rutgers, Robeson had been involved in a relationship with a young African-American woman named Geraldine Maimie Neale. The two cared deeply about each other, yet when Robeson asked her to marry him as he approached his graduation from college, Neale said no. She knew that Robeson would always have interests that went beyond his marriage and family. Robeson was someone who felt strongly about making a difference in the lives of America's black men and women.

In fact, Neale was not the only one who believed Robeson was destined for greatness. Each graduating class at Rutgers made predictions about the future of the students. According to the class prophecy, Robeson would one day become governor of New Jersey and would become a leader of America's African-American citizens.

Robeson was not sure of what lay in store for him. While he was figuring it out, he planned to attend Columbia University Law School in New York. Robeson's father had hoped his son would follow in his footsteps and

PAUL ROBESON

become a minister. Yet Robeson believed he could be of more service to African Americans as a lawyer.

In the summer of 1919, the twenty-one-year-old Robeson arrived in Harlem, New York, an African-American community. The move was easy for him. His name was well known in the area because of his college football career. The people of Harlem—just like his friends and family in New Jersey—knew him, liked him, and were proud of him.

In order to earn money so he could attend law school, Robeson returned to New Jersey every weekend to tutor his college football coach's son in Latin. He brought in more money by helping coach the football team at Lincoln University, playing on a practice team against the varsity squad of Columbia University, and when time allowed, playing professionally for the Akron Pros and the Milwaukee Badgers.

Robeson's thigh muscle was injured during one of the games, and he had to be rushed to the hospital where he was operated on immediately. The injury was a severe one. Even though the operation was successful, Robeson spent several weeks in the hospital in a great deal of pain.

A doctor at the hospital became friendly with Robeson and decided to introduce him to Eslanda "Essie" Goode, an African-American pathology technician who worked there.

COLLEGE AND CAREER CHOICES

> ### Unfair Treatment in the Akron Pros
> During the time that Robeson played for the Akron Pros, the team had a streak of eighteen games without a loss. Robeson was paid a thousand dollars a game but had to deal with a lot of prejudice. The team's fans insulted him when he played, and he had to change into his uniform in the team owner's cigar factory. On the road, Robeson was unable to get a hotel room or eat in the restaurants with the other white players.

Intelligent and energetic, Goode had grown up in Washington, D.C., before moving to New York. She had attended the University of Illinois on a scholarship and then finished her studies at Columbia University. When she went to work at New York's Presbyterian Hospital, she was the first African American hired for a staff position.

Robeson and Goode got along very well, although they had very different personalities. Robeson was an easygoing young man who generally liked most people. Goode trusted very few people and had no trouble letting people know when she did not like them. Goode liked to wake up early and start her day. She had regular meals at a set time and made definite plans for each day. Robeson preferred waking up late and eating his meals at no particular time.

The two began seeing a lot of each other. "[I]t was clear that he [Paul] was an extraordinary figure—a man of

PAUL ROBESON

A football injury brought together Robeson and his wife Eslanda.

COLLEGE AND CAREER CHOICES

. . . intelligence and talent," Goode said about first meeting him.[3]

Yet Robeson had not forgotten Gerry Neale, the young woman he had proposed to in college. He visited Neale a few times over the next couple years, making it clear that he still wanted to marry her. Neale refused his offer each time. Meanwhile, Goode was sure that she wanted to marry Robeson and that the two of them would make a good couple. She made sure to run into him whenever possible, she read up on subjects that she knew were of interest to him, especially sports, and she arranged her schedule so she could walk home from Columbia University with him.

Her plan, combined with Neale's refusal to marry Robeson, worked. On August 17, 1921, Robeson asked Goode to marry him. He said they should go out and do it that day. They first headed to Greenwich, Connecticut, where they could get married quickly and without a ceremony. But they were told that since they came from New York and were not Connecticut residents, they would have to wait five days. On the train ride back to New York, the couple saw a sign advertising a town clerk who could marry them. They got off the train, visited the town clerk, and were pronounced husband and wife a few minutes later.

Essie Robeson worked at the hospital while Robeson continued attending law school and playing football.

PAUL ROBESON

Robeson was able to bring in some extra money with occasional singing performances. He had also acted since 1920 with the Amateur Players, a group of African-American students. Not long after his marriage, Robeson was asked to play the lead in *Simon the Cyrenian* at the Harlem YWCA. Although Robeson did not take his performance seriously, there were some people in the theater business who watched him and liked what they saw. Robeson was asked to act professionally in the play *Taboo*; he would have the lead role. Robeson was more interested in getting his law degree than pursuing a career in acting. But eventually—with Essie urging him—he agreed to take the role as long as he could continue going to law school at the same time.

"He didn't want to be an actor, but how high could he go in his [law] profession?" Essie said. "This was America and he was a Negro; therefore he wouldn't get far. If he put his foot on the bottom rung of the ladder of the theater, he could climb to the top."[4]

The plot of *Taboo* was centered on a southern plantation and the slaves who worked there. Robeson would play the part of a wandering minstrel who at one point turns into a voodoo king.

The play only lasted four performances in New York and the reviews were mixed. Yet friends who saw Robeson perform urged him to pursue an acting career.

COLLEGE AND CAREER CHOICES

"I knew little of what I was doing, but I was urged to go ahead and try," said Robeson. "So I found myself in rehearsal. What was most important at that time was that I got about $75 a week, which a law clerk didn't get for quite some time . . . The first night after I'd played the role, I came back to the Law School . . . I hadn't seen the papers, and I—well—I was fairly famous."[5]

Socialite Mary Hoyt Wilborg was a wealthy woman who decided to put on a production of *Taboo* in London. Again, Robeson was asked to be in the show.

If Robeson still had doubts about performing on stage, his wife did not. She thought that the color of his skin would matter less to the theater world than it would in the world of law. She thought Robeson would have a better chance of success as an actor and so she convinced him to travel to London with the production.

Before sailing for England, Robeson landed a role in a Broadway hit called *Shuffle Along*. The musical was an African-American production featuring an African-American quartet called The Four Harmony Kings. The group's bass singer left without giving notice and Robeson was asked to take his place. Although Robeson tripped onstage and almost fell down, he remained on his feet to sing "Old Black Joe." The audience applauded wildly.

> If Robeson still had doubts about performing on stage, his wife did not.

33

PAUL ROBESON

Robeson spent part of the summer of 1922 in London, acting in *Taboo*. The night before he was scheduled to sail to England, Essie became sick. She had had her appendix removed years earlier and now needed to be operated on again. Not wanting to worry her husband, since he was about to sail across the Atlantic Ocean, she did not tell him. She waved good-bye as his ship sailed away and wrote twenty-one letters. She gave them to friends who would mail one letter to Robeson every few days.

After the operation, Essie was very ill and had to stay in the hospital longer than expected. Meanwhile, the production was not going well in England. Robeson had hoped his wife would come over and join him but since the play was not doing well, he wrote to her that he was not sure what to do. Her letters, of course, did not provide any answers since Essie was still in the hospital and had written her letters before Robeson had even arrived in England.

Finally, after Essie had been recovering in the hospital for more than a month, she sent Robeson a telegram about her condition. He was upset that she had not told him about her illness before and he was very worried about her. Since the play was not doing well anyway, he decided to sail home.

As soon as Robeson's ship docked, he went directly to the hospital to see Essie. He stayed by her side for the next few weeks, and soon she was able to go home.

COLLEGE AND CAREER CHOICES

As always, money was tight, especially since Robeson had to pay for his last year of law school. He took a variety of jobs to help pay expenses. He spent some time at Rutgers working with Coach Sanford and the football team. He also performed at a few concerts and he accepted a role in the chorus of the *Plantation Revue*. Robeson found a job working in the post office, and he played professional football again. At one point, he was approached about being trained as a boxer who would fight against Jack Dempsey, who won the world heavyweight title in the 1920s. But Robeson turned down the offer. He had no interest in becoming a prize fighter. He did, however, want to get his law degree.

Robeson finally received his law degree in February 1923. Louis William Stotesbury, a Rutgers graduate, offered him a job in his firm. In late spring, Robeson began working there, the only black American on the staff. Although he worked hard, he seemed to encounter prejudice at every turn. Robeson needed a secretary to assist him with something, and she refused because he was black. When Robeson talked to Stotesbury, he was told that he would probably never be able to rise very high in the legal profession. The fact of the matter

> Robeson needed a secretary to assist him with something, and she refused because he was black.

PAUL ROBESON

was that in 1923, few white clients would be willing to have an African-American lawyer.

Robeson had always aimed high. If he could not succeed as a lawyer, he would leave the profession. He resigned from the firm. The question was: What would he do now?

Chapter 4

On Stage

Robeson received a letter one day in the fall of 1923 from Kenneth Macgowan. Macgowan was the director of the Provincetown Players. The actors would be putting on a new play called *All God's Chillun Got Wings* by the famous American playwright Eugene O'Neill. Robeson was being considered for a part.

Eager for work, Robeson showed up for his audition at the Provincetown Playhouse. Bess Rockmore, who worked as an assistant to the director, said of his audition, "All I remember is . . . this marvelous, incredible voice . . . I can tell you he was a most impressive personality . . . He was built so beautifully. He moved so gracefully."[1]

All God's Chillun Got Wings had problems from the start. It had to be postponed a number of times for various reasons, including contract disputes, poor health on the part of one of the actors, and the controversial plot.

PAUL ROBESON

All God's Chillun Got Wings

The story of *All God's Chillun Got Wings* told of the relationship between a black man and a white woman, an idea that was not acceptable to many Americans in the early twentieth century. Although laws had been passed since the end of the Civil War to make sure African Americans were treated fairly, that did not mean the majority of white people thought of them as equal. The two races were kept segregated, or separate, in most public places such as schools, restaurants, and movies.

Long before the play was scheduled to open, people were reacting violently to the story line. Newspaper articles appeared regularly describing how upset much of the public was about the play. Plus, the theater received obscene letters aimed at the actors—especially Robeson—and even an anonymous bomb threat.

Meanwhile, while Robeson was waiting for the play to go into production, he performed songs written by African-American composers at the Brooklyn YWCA. He also attended various banquets where he was asked to sing and was even approached by a record company. He also appeared for a couple weeks in the play *Roseanne*, performing in the production in both New York and Philadelphia.

Once rehearsals began for *All God's Chillun Got Wings*, everyone involved was aware of the tension surrounding

ON STAGE

the show. Fearing a riot—or worse—when the play opened, the people who ran the theater decided to take some of the attention off the show by reviving another O'Neill play, *The Emperor Jones*. This play would open on May 6 while *All God's Chillun Got Wings* would open nine days later. Robeson was asked to play the part of Brutus Jones, the lead role in *The Emperor Jones*, and he had two weeks to learn his lines before the show opened. At the same time, he had to have his part—also a lead—memorized for *All God's Chillun Got Wings*.

Essie helped her husband memorize his lines for *The Emperor Jones*. With the script in her hands, she worked with Robeson all through the day and night, even during meals and when they were getting ready to go to bed. Robeson pored over the lines just as he had done years ago, when his father helped him prepare a speech. He went through the script word by word, "digging down to the meaning of every single comma," Essie said.[2]

Essie and Robeson also made themselves use lines from the script in their everyday life, to help Robeson memorize the part. For example, if Robeson was awakened in the middle of the night by some noise, instead of saying, "What was that? What woke me up?" he would say one of his lines, "Who dare whistle dat way in my palace? Who dare wake up de emperor?"[3]

The experience was challenging but also extremely rewarding for Robeson. *The Emperor Jones* opened in May.

PAUL ROBESON

Robeson played Jim in *All God's Chillun Got Wings*.

ON STAGE

Both the audience and the theater critics praised the production. On opening night, Robeson was called out five times to take a bow. The reviews in the newspapers commented on the power and richness of Robeson's voice and of the strong emotions he brought to the part.

When *All God's Chillun Got Wings* opened several days later, the mood was tense. The theater was surrounded by police in case violence broke out. Robeson and his wife took different streets from those they normally traveled to get to the theater, in case people were waiting to harm them. In addition to the threat of violence that hovered over the theater, the producers had another dilemma. In the early 1920s, any theater that wanted to hire children to play parts had to get permission from the city's mayor. New York's mayor, James Hylan, had just given approval to another show that was using a seven-year-old child in it. Yet he turned down the Provincetown Players' request to use a few children who were eleven years old through seventeen years old in their opening scene.

When Robeson walked onto the stage, he said he "half expected to hear shots from the stalls."[4]

But there were no shots and no trouble. Since there could be no children in the opening scene, which called for black and white children to be playing together, James Light stood on stage and read the opening scene out loud to the audience.

PAUL ROBESON

Lawrence Brown was Robeson's longtime singing partner.

ON STAGE

After all the buildup, the play did not receive great reviews. Yet Robeson was praised and called a great actor by the critics. *All God's Chillun Got Wings* and *The Emperor Jones* ran through June; then *All God's Chillun Got Wings* ran for another few months by itself. Robeson did not earn a lot of money from these roles; his entire salary for both shows came to slightly more than fifteen hundred dollars.

Robeson performed at public and private concerts, and he also starred in a movie made by an African-American filmmaker. The movie was called *Body and Soul* and Robeson played a corrupt pastor in it. When *The Emperor Jones* opened on Broadway, Robeson repeated his starring role.

Robeson also began working with black musician Lawrence Brown. Brown sang and played the piano, and he practiced with Robeson on a daily basis. The two men concentrated on African-American spirituals—songs that originated with African Americans in the South—and finally performed the songs one night at the home of a friend. All the guests were very impressed with the two men and urged them to give a public concert. The Provincetown Players offered their theater as the setting for Brown's arrangements and Robeson's outstanding voice.

"I'm pretty young and for the present I can do no better than to do my own work and develop myself to the best of my ability," said Robeson. "It was a happy fate that connected me with the Provincetown for just this."[5]

The concert was advertised in the newspapers and held on April 19, 1925. So many people had been talking about it that, on the night of the performance, the theater was packed. People were turned away because there was no room for them to sit down. Many decided just to stand in the wings, so at least they could hear the music. The men sang spirituals like "Steal Away" and "Joshua Fit de Battle of Jericho." The evening was a huge success. Brown and Robeson were asked to give sixteen encores and were only able to leave the stage when the lights were turned up in the theater.

For Robeson, the experience was extremely rewarding. "No one can hear these songs as our people sang them and not understand the Negro a little better," Robeson said. "I found that on the stage, whether singing or acting, race and color prejudices are forgotten. Art is the one form against which such barriers do not stand, and I think it is through art we are going to come into our own."[6]

In August, the twenty-seven-year-old Robeson sailed to England with Essie. He was set to perform in the London production of *The Emperor Jones*, which was opening there in the fall.

"I honestly feel that my future depends mostly upon myself," said Robeson. "My courage in fighting over the rough places that are bound to come—my eagerness to

ON STAGE

work and learn—my constant realization that I have always a few steps more to go—perhaps never realizing the desired perfection—but plugging away."[7]

The Robesons were pleasantly surprised to find how easily accepted they were in London. When Essie found an apartment for the two of them to rent during their stay, the landlord did not offer any objections to renting it to African Americans.

"I learned that there truly is a kinship among us all, a basis for mutual respect and brotherly love," said Robeson. "My first glimpse of this concept came through song, and that is not strange, for the songs that have lived through the years have always been the purest expressions of the heart of humanity."[8]

After the first performance of *The Emperor Jones*, Essie said:

> Well, it was a great night. All day Paul and I were just loafing around the house. I played pinochle with him, and chatted to ease him up . . . The house was packed with the most wonderful audience. When Paul stepped out on the stage yawning, there was terrific applause, a real personal triumph before he had done a thing . . . Paul was magnificent.[9]

Robeson received excellent reviews but said, "I couldn't understand what they were talking about. I knew nothing about the technique of acting, or about the actor's art."[10]

Soon Robeson's name was lit up on marquees. Yet the play itself was not favorably reviewed, and after five weeks it closed. But when Robeson took his bows after the last

PAUL ROBESON

Robeson was a great stage and screen presence in *The Emperor Jones*.

ON STAGE

performance, the audience rose to its feet and applauded wildly.

Robeson and his wife stayed in London even after *The Emperor Jones* was no longer running. They enjoyed the city and the freedom of movement they had there. Robeson also started voice training with Flora Arnold, a vocal coach.

Determined to find some time for Robeson to rest, Essie arranged for the two of them to take a vacation in France. The couple traveled to Paris and met such famous authors as Ernest Hemingway, Gertrude Stein, and James Joyce. After several weeks of travel, the Robesons set sail for home.

Back in New York, Robeson immediately had to get ready for several concerts with Lawrence Brown that their agent had set up. Robeson performed in New York, Detroit, Indianapolis, Philadelphia, and Pittsburgh. The concerts were well-received by audiences and critics, and, at the same time, the recordings of these spirituals sold well. The most popular record had "Joshua Fit de Battle of Jericho" on one side and "Bye and Bye" on the other.

Robeson made more recordings for the Victor Company in the winter of 1926. Poet Langston Hughes listened to the records and was so moved by what he heard that he wrote to Robeson: "The great truth and beauty of your art struck me as never before."[11]

Chapter 5

Beyond the United States

When Robeson resumed the concert tour in February 1926, there were difficulties with the performances. In Chicago, he was set to sing at Orchestra Hall, which could house a large audience. But there had been few advertisements for the performance, and so the turnout was small, even though Robeson gave one of his best recitals.

Poor attendance was again the problem in Green Bay and Milwaukee, Wisconsin. The following month, Robeson appeared in Boston. This time, there was no saving the performance. Robeson had come down with a bad cold a few days before the concert. He stayed in bed and did not even want to go on at the Copley Plaza, one of the best hotels in Boston. However, Lawrence Brown and Essie talked him into performing. Although Robeson

BEYOND THE UNITED STATES

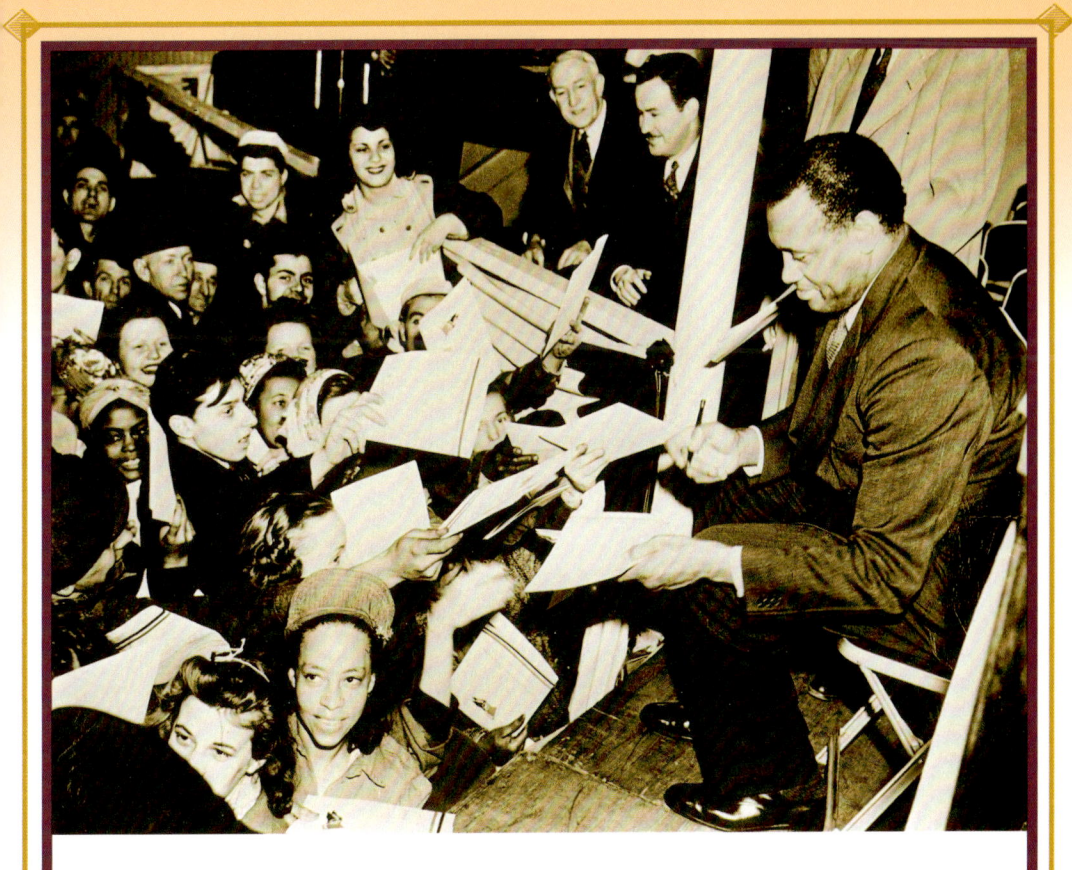

Robeson soon became a famous entertainer and often signed autographs.

made it through all the songs, he did not sing well. His voice was tight and he did not sound like himself.

Robeson knew he had performed poorly and it upset him. For the past couple of years, he had experienced nothing but praise and success. Now, he suddenly became worried about his future as a singer. He had frequent problems with his throat and voice, and he was not sure what to

PAUL ROBESON

do. Essie suggested he talk to a voice teacher and he took her advice. He began working with Teresa Armitage, a music teacher with the Chicago school district, and he also spoke with a doctor who took care of a growth Robeson had on his vocal cords.

During the summer, Robeson was asked to play the lead in *Black Boy*, a story based on the life of Jack Johnson, an African-American prizefighter. The play received poor reviews and did not stay in production very long. Yet the critics praised Robeson, claiming that his performance in *Black Boy* was even better than the work he did in *The Emperor Jones*.

A couple of months after the show closed, Robeson went on the road with Brown. The musicians traveled through the Midwest giving concerts. In Kansas City, a small group of African Americans had gotten together to organize a concert company. They did not think they would be able to pay the usual fee Robeson charged, which was $1,250 a night for a place the size of Kansas City. In an effort to support the work the group was doing, Robeson said he would accept a salary of $750. Not many tickets were sold ahead of time because the advertisements stated that there would not be separate seating for whites and blacks. Robeson reassured the concert company that no matter how poor attendance might be, "I will sing for my people."[1]

BEYOND THE UNITED STATES

Yet a crowd did turn out and the company made a profit, even after Robeson was paid. "I am not ashamed of the Spirituals," said Robeson. "They represent the soul of my people. White and colored people react alike to the songs. Differences are forgotten and prejudices vanish when mixed audiences meet at the concerts. Humanity is helped and lifted to higher levels."[2]

Robeson toured Europe with Brown in the fall of 1927. Essie was pregnant. While he was away, his son, Paul Robeson, Jr., was born on November 2, 1927. Essie became ill after the baby was born, but she kept this news from Robeson in her letters, just as she had several years earlier. Yet when Robeson finally learned of Essie's condition six weeks later, he immediately sailed home.

Back in the United States, Robeson took the part of Crown in the play *Porgy*. For six weeks, he earned five hundred dollars in the show and then moved on to *Show Boat*, a musical that had been a huge success in New York and would soon be opening in London. In the part of Joe, Robeson would sing "Ol' Man River"—and no other song. There would be little wear and tear on his voice and he would be featured in a first-rate production. Robeson enthusiastically accepted the offer.

So he headed back to England. When the musical opened, most of the critics gave it rave reviews. Yet even those who were not thrilled with the production thought Robeson did a superb job in his role of Joe. "People went

PAUL ROBESON

> ### Other Women
> Throughout the years of their marriage, Robeson's relationship with his wife would go up and down. Many women—especially actresses—were attracted to Robeson and, in many cases, he returned the interest. Yet even though he spent time with other women over the years, Robeson stayed married to Essie.

out of their minds about him," said actor Bernard Sarron.[3]

The show was a financial success and Essie was able to join Robeson in London not long after it opened.

While Robeson was performing in *Show Boat* in the evenings, he was often giving afternoon recitals with Brown. After one of these concerts, the Prince of Wales was so impressed that he arranged for a performance in honor of the king of Spain. Not only did the Robesons meet royalty, but they became friendly with such celebrated writers of the day as H. G. Wells, who wrote *The Time Machine* and *The War of the Worlds*, and George Bernard Shaw who wrote *Pygmalion*.

Show Boat ran until March 1929. Remaining in Europe after the musical closed, Robeson continued giving recitals and he also traveled to other European countries. During his travels, Robeson took a great interest in Russian and Slavonic folk songs. He felt they were similar to the Negro spirituals—all these folk songs seemed to tell of a sorrow of the people. Robeson became interested in learning about the hardships many ethnic groups in Europe had faced through the years, particularly the Jews.

BEYOND THE UNITED STATES

Robeson's performances in concerts when he returned to England were nothing short of incredible. Tickets for his performance at Albert Hall sold out and critics raved about his singing. He also spent much of his time taking voice lessons and learning foreign languages.

When Robeson returned to the United States, he went on a huge concert tour throughout the country. His career was now being handled by F. C. Coppicus of the

Paul Robeson sits on the shoulders of students in Prague, Czechoslovakia. Today, Prague is in the Czech Republic.

PAUL ROBESON

Metropolitan Music Bureau, and his first appearance in November 1929 was at Carnegie Hall in New York City. Although he did not sing his best that first night—and the critics let him know it—he performed wonderfully there five nights later. Tickets sold so well that one thousand people had to be turned away. Robeson learned from the ushers that no performer at Carnegie Hall had ever played to a sold-out crowd twice in five days.

Pleased as Robeson was with the attendance at his concerts, he was not generally pleased with American audiences. Compared to theatergoers in England, Robeson felt American crowds were merely interested in an evening of entertainment rather than a true love of the theater. In short, he felt the English were more cultured than the Americans. He also felt far more self-conscious about the color of his skin in his native land.

When Robeson was thirty, he traveled once again to London to play a part he had often thought about: Othello. The Shakespearean tragedy of the same name tells the story of a black Moor who elopes with Desdemona, a fair-skinned woman.

Before beginning rehearsal, Robeson went on two tours where he gave concerts throughout Europe. He also appeared in a movie, *Borderline*, in Switzerland. It was an experimental film and it was silent, as were most films at this time. Essie appeared in the film as well.

BEYOND THE UNITED STATES

Robeson sometimes sang spirituals at churches.

PAUL ROBESON

Following the filming, the couple's next stop was Berlin, Germany, where Robeson took part in two performances of *The Emperor Jones*. Jimmy Light, of the Provincetown Players, was directing the production and Robeson was glad for the chance to work with him again, even for such a short time.

By April, Robeson was back in London to rehearse *Othello*. He was nervous about playing such a demanding role. The director, Nellie Van Volkenburg, had never directed one of Shakespeare's plays. With little instruction, the actors focused on helping one another—sometimes meeting together at different homes so they could rehearse. Jimmy Light also came to Robeson's aid and helped him with the part.

The inexperienced Van Volkenburg made a mess of the staging and the sets. She even cut some of the script so that she could put in dance and music scenes. The lighting was so dim, that the audience could barely see the actors. Robeson's costume consisted of Elizabethan tights and puffed sleeves rather than the flowing robes of a Moor. Not surprisingly, Robeson was very nervous when opening night arrived.

Yet the audience loved him. When the curtain fell, Robeson was called out twenty times to take bows. "I'm so happy. I'm so happy," he said.[4]

BEYOND THE UNITED STATES

The play itself was heavily criticized and not all reviewers praised Robeson's performance. Other critics, however, called him a natural in the Shakespearean role, claiming he played the part with dignity and passion.

Throughout the run of *Othello*, Robeson kept working with Light, always trying to put in a better performance. The play lasted six weeks. At this time, Essie's biography of Robeson—*Paul Robeson, Negro*—was published. Reviews of the book were generally good, but it did not sell well.

In 1931, Robeson went to work again with director Jimmy Light, this time in the London production of Eugene O'Neill's *The Hairy Ape*. Robeson had long suffered from throat problems, and his voice now was a matter of huge concern. He was straining his throat and, in general, felt physically exhausted partly because he had finished another concert tour before appearing in *The Hairy Ape*.

The Hairy Ape closed after five performances because Robeson was near collapse. He had laryngitis and was too tired to do anything but go to bed. A doctor kept him in a nursing home for a week and this helped Robeson get over the physical and nervous strain. This would be the first time—but by no means the last—that Robeson would be overwhelmed by physical problems.

Chapter 6

The Spell of the Soviet Union

Robeson was ready to undertake another concert tour of the United States at the start of 1932. By this time, Robeson had been studying the Russian language for a while and developing an ever-increasing appreciation of their folk songs. On the tour, he added for the first time some songs that were not Negro spirituals, such as "The Captive" by Gretchaninov and a Russian prayer.

"He feels he is a kindred soul," wrote Emma Goldman about Robeson's feelings toward the Russian people. "I can't tell you how beautiful he talks Russian."[1]

The Russian songs were received enthusiastically by audiences, and Robeson was pleased. It was the content of the folk songs—rather than the melodies—that interested

THE SPELL OF THE SOVIET UNION

him. He felt the Russians and African Americans had much in common.

The concert tour lasted two months. In the spring, Robeson appeared on Broadway in a revival of the Kern and Hammerstein musical *Show Boat*. The strong performers selected for the show resulted in outstanding reviews from the critics—and Robeson's own reviews had never been better. A short version of the music was broadcast over the radio and this, too, was praised.

"The show has gone splendidly and I'm really *singing* the *song*," Robeson wrote to his wife. "Marvelous reviews. This country is *really* mine. And strange, I like it again and deeply. After all—this audience understands the Negro in a way impossible for Europeans."[2]

At this time, Robeson was presented with an honorary master of arts degree from Rutgers. The president of Princeton University also received the honorary degree at this time to Robeson's amusement. At the time Robeson was enrolling in college, Princeton did not admit African Americans.

Robeson had been traveling back and forth between England and the United States for many years, both for his career and personal reasons. Although it was not always easy, he tried to spend as much time as he could with his five-year-old son.

"One of my first and best memories of him [Robeson] comes from this week, when he took me to see Peter Pan

PAUL ROBESON

Robeson acted in many versions of the musical *Show Boat*. Here he is playing "Joe" in the Drury Lane Theatre production of the show in London in 1928.

THE SPELL OF THE SOVIET UNION

". . . and softly talked me through the scary parts, holding my hand and helping me deal with my fear of Captain Hook and the crocodile," said Pauli.[3]

In the winter of 1933, Robeson was back in England getting ready for a production of *All God's Chillun Got Wings*. The show was a success but had to close after two months because Robeson was due back in New York to shoot a movie version of *The Emperor Jones*.

The Emperor Jones was the first movie with sound that Robeson had ever appeared in. He put in six weeks on the set and was fifteen thousand dollars wealthier for his efforts.

Ever since he had been a boy, Robeson had been aware of the importance of taking pride in his heritage. This feeling of pride had grown over the years, and Robeson now began expressing his ideas—privately and publicly—

The Emperor Jones

Robeson enjoyed making the film *The Emperor Jones*. He was particularly interested in acting in stories that steered away from African Americans on plantations. He was interested in scripts that fully represented the lives of black people. Robeson was beginning to find a lot wrong with life in America. He felt there was not enough focus on black culture and that its traditions were greater than those of white America and should be made known.

about the need to understand African heritage. He wanted to inform the rest of the country of African-American traditions.

One of the first things he did was to start studying various African languages. "I want to find out things for myself," said Robeson, "and see the country from where my ancestors came. Anything that can be done to show that the African Negro had some cultural background will help the movement."[4]

After learning languages of groups on Africa's East Coast, he studied Ewe, Efik, and Hausa, languages of the West Coast and Bantu, which was where his own family had originated. Robeson also listened to recordings of each culture's folk songs. He believed strongly that although the black people in the United States should contribute to the white culture, they should be careful to preserve their own identity.

Robeson said that the black man must have the "courage to follow his own way. He can't be Chinese, Arabian, European, or anything else. He must be African."[5]

Concentrating much of his energy on these ideas, Robeson was excited when he was asked to appear in the movie *Sanders of the River*. Zoltan Korda, a Hungarian film director known for his adventure stories, was making the movie and he had already spent nearly half a year putting the music, speech, dance, and customs of Central Africa on

THE SPELL OF THE SOVIET UNION

Robeson poses for a portrait in London.

PAUL ROBESON

film. Robeson was sure that this film footage would help people throughout the world better understand African traditions and culture.

The movie, however, turned out differently. The theme came across as the need for white men to tame the native Africans. Robeson believed it made Africans look childish and dependent on whites. Yet he defended taking the part.

"To expect the Negro artist to reject every role with which he is not . . . in agreement, is to expect him under our present scheme of things to give up his work entirely—unless of course he is to confine himself solely to the left theater," Robeson said.[6]

The film left Robeson as dissatisfied as ever with life in the United States and western society in general. "I did it all in the name of art . . . I hate the picture," he said.[7]

When Soviet filmmaker Sergei Eisenstein invited Robeson to visit the Soviet Union, Robeson accepted. Eisenstein was planning to make a film about Toussaint-L'Ouverture, a former revolutionary leader in Haiti. Robeson headed to Moscow in the winter of 1934 to discuss the movie.

He took a train from London to Moscow and found himself in Berlin, Germany, during the trip. Germany in the 1930s was a dangerous place. The country was now under the leadership of Adolf Hitler and the Nazi party. Racism and anti-Semitism were rampant and Robeson was

THE SPELL OF THE SOVIET UNION

an unwelcome visitor. When Nazi storm troopers began yelling at Robeson at the train station in Berlin, Robeson grew tense, expecting the fight to become physical.

Fortunately, the train pulled out before violence erupted. Robeson was very relieved to get out of Germany, and he arrived safely in Moscow, along with Essie and Marie Seton.

From the start, Robeson seemed to fall under the spell of Russia. He, Essie, and Seton were greeted warmly by the filmmaker Sergei Eisenstein, playwright Alexander Afinogenov, some Soviet officials, and some African Americans who were living in the Soviet Union. Essie's brothers were also living in Russia and greeted their sister and Robeson warmly. Robeson spoke Russian well and people were overjoyed to hear him talk in their native tongue. Their two-week stay was filled with banquets, numerous trips to the theater, and visits to local hospitals, factories, and centers for children.

"I feel like a human being for the first time since I grew up," said Robeson.[8]

Robeson and Essie were so pleased with what they saw of Soviet life, that they considered sending their son Pauli to school there. He lived most of the time with Essie's mother in New York. Robeson liked the idea of his son being raised in Russia, where he sensed little, if any, prejudice against black people.

PAUL ROBESON

Robeson poses with his only son, Paul Jr.

THE SPELL OF THE SOVIET UNION

When Robeson returned to England, he went on a concert tour that included Scotland, Wales, and Ireland. His goal now was to earn enough money over the next year or two so he could devote himself to becoming politically active. Robeson was ever in search of a better way of life, a life where there was no prejudice and all people were treated equally.

"Sometimes I think I am the only Negro living who would not prefer to be white," said Robeson.

> It has been said that I am to leave Europe to go back among my own people. This does not mean that I am to abandon my career. Though I shall visit Africa . . . I shall return to Europe. Where I live is not important. But I am going back to my people in the sense that for the rest of my life I am going to think and feel as an African—not as a white man.[9]

Because of Robeson's awakening interest in politics and the fact that he often voiced his thoughts publicly, some people close to him worried that few people would attend his concerts. However, large crowds poured into the concert halls to hear Robeson perform. Just as he had done in the past, his program focused on Negro spirituals. Audiences loved him—and for more than his voice. When Robeson sang, his emotions came through and the crowds responded to the strong feelings he expressed when singing songs of his African heritage.

Robeson agreed to play the part of Toussaint L'Ouverture in a play in London and to once again appear as Joe in the movie version of *Show Boat*. Although *Show*

PAUL ROBESON

Boat did not fit in with any of his current political interests, Robeson still was interested in earning good money and he was offered forty thousand dollars for his role in the movie. After visiting their son who was staying with his grandmother, Robeson and Essie traveled to Hollywood, California, to shoot the movie in the fall of 1935.

Once the Robesons arrived in Hollywood, Robeson spent two months there making the movie. Director James Whale worked with the actor on how to be comfortable in front of the camera and how to get the most out of his voice. Robeson relaxed and gave an enthusiastic performance of "Ol' Man River." When the song was over, the musicians in the orchestra applauded him.

Robeson returned to London a few months later to begin rehearsals for the play about Toussaint L'Ouverture. As had happened frequently throughout his career, Robeson was praised by the critics, although the play itself received disappointing notices.

Robeson next decided to accept a role in the film *Song of Freedom*. He was to play the role of John Zinga, a dockworker in London, who goes on to have a great singing career. Once he becomes famous, Zinga travels to Africa where he tries to educate the people there. Robeson was enthusiastic about the movie because unlike *Show Boat*, *Song of Freedom* presented the black man as a real human being.

THE SPELL OF THE SOVIET UNION

Robeson poses with his costar from *Song of Freedom*.

The movie "gives me a real part for the first time," Robeson said.[10]

The year 1936 was Robeson's busiest ever. Once he had finished *Song of Freedom*, Robeson moved on to *King Solomon's Mines*. But before he started shooting the movie, Robeson decided to take a short vacation—back to the Soviet Union.

Chapter 7

Political Interests

Robeson stayed on a collective farm while he visited Russia. He loved the experience and was pleasantly surprised at how much the children there seemed to know about the hardships black men and black women faced in the United States. Robeson now felt certain that Pauli should be raised and educated in Russia.

Robeson went to work on *King Solomon's Mines* when he returned from Russia. It was an elaborate production complete with thousands of "natives" and erupting volcanoes. When filming was over, Robeson wanted to find a way of thanking the studio technicians for their help. They had asked to hear him sing, so Robeson had a grand piano brought to the set, and he put on a spur-of-the-moment concert for the technicians.

POLITICAL INTERESTS

> ### Soviet Schooling
> Robeson was warned by a friend to tell newspaper reporters that Pauli would be sent to school in Russia. The friend had enrolled his own son in a school in Moscow—only to have the Soviet government tell him he could not take the boy out. The more public Robeson made his decision, the less likely he was to have any trouble if he chose to remove Pauli.

On another occasion, "after a long train trip, he walked the length of the train to thank the crew personally, shake their hands, and chat," said his son, Pauli.[1]

The film did not present blacks in a very dignified way and Robeson hoped that his next movie, *Big Fella*, would be a work he was proud of. The movie was based on the story of "Banjo," by Claude McKay. Robeson asked the writers to make some changes in the script so that Banjo, the lead character, was a more reliable and trustworthy man. Also, the name of the movie was changed from *Banjo* to *Big Fella* so that the audience would not automatically think of cotton plantations and poor black men. Essie and Larry Brown also had roles in the film.

Robeson had plenty of work as he approached his fortieth birthday. The movie *Jericho* would be his next production. But first, he went back to Russia for a month. He helped Pauli and Essie's mother move in to their new

PAUL ROBESON

Robeson brought a strong performance to the film *King Solomon's Mines*.

POLITICAL INTERESTS

home and he also went on a concert tour. Pauli was enrolled in a Soviet school. Robeson was very excited about his son being educated in Russia where—according to Robeson—there was practically no prejudice or discrimination. Pauli would remain in Russia for nearly two years.

Jericho was being filmed in Egypt. Robeson and Essie traveled to the city of Cairo for a month. Some of the scenes were filmed near the pyramids. One day, Robeson, an interpreter, and a couple of people involved in the movie visited the center of the pyramid with only the smallest amount of lighting to guide them. At the center, they realized there was a large echo and they asked Robeson to sing.

The first note Robeson sang "almost crumbled the place," said Henry Wilcoxon, an actor in the film.[2] Robeson sang "Oh Isis und Osiris" from Mozart's opera *The Magic Flute*. When he finished the beautiful performance, everyone in the group was crying—even Robeson himself.

"There were tears going down our faces," said Wilcoxon. "And we almost daren't breathe to break the spell of the thing."[3]

Robeson traveled to Russia for the summer. He was pleased with Pauli's life there and Pauli was happy to spend time with his father. Robeson was especially pleased at the way he believed minority groups were treated in Russia.

PAUL ROBESON

He believed they were treated fairly while at the same time, they were encouraged to preserve their own culture and traditions.

After spending the summer in Russia, Robeson became more politically involved. He began to give concerts and make appearances in support of the Republic in the Spanish Civil War. The war lasted from 1936 until 1939, and supporters of the Republic saw the struggle as a battle against a dictatorship. In addition to making numerous public appearances, Robeson wanted to travel to Spain and see for himself what was happening there. He wanted to do as much as he could to support the Republic. So he visited such cities as Barcelona, Tarazona, and Madrid. He sang for the soldiers and they, in turn, could not believe Robeson had traveled to the war-torn country on their behalf. Robeson met with troops wherever he went; everyone recognized him. In Tarazona, fifteen hundred soldiers from a dozen countries crowded into a church to hear Robeson sing.

> In Tarazona, fifteen hundred soldiers from a dozen countries crowded into a church to hear Robeson sing.

From Tarazona, Robeson was allowed to enter Madrid because he had been given government papers. The city had been bombed daily for months and neither women nor children were able to enter the city. In Madrid, Robeson met with Communist leaders and he also visited soldiers who had been fighting on the front line.

POLITICAL INTERESTS

When Robeson and Essie left Spain to cross over into France, army captain Fernando Castillo took off the medal for heroism, which he had been given in 1936. "I give you this," he said to Essie, who gratefully accepted the medal.[4]

"I have never met such courage in a people," said Robeson.[5]

By this time, the situation in Europe was very unsettled. The world was on the brink of war and Robeson did not want Pauli to remain in the Russian school. Pauli, now ten, went to live with his parents in England, while his grandmother went to the United States. He was, however, enrolled in a Soviet school in London where Russian officials sent their children. This way, he could continue with an academic program similar to the one he had been studying in Moscow.

Robeson started rehearsing for the play *Plant in the Sun* while he was in London. The play was put on by the Unity Theatre, a political group that aimed at presenting productions that would highlight the lives and hardships of the typical worker. Robeson turned to this group with interest. He was determined to appear only in shows that brought to light the problems of average people.

Robeson had changed his way of thinking. He used to believe in the "talented tenth" theory, just as most people involved in the Harlem Renaissance did. The theory held that the best and brightest—or top 10 percent—of African

PAUL ROBESON

Americans could uplift the rest of the race. But Robeson no longer felt this way.

Plant in the Sun told the story of black and white workers at a candy factory joining together to strike against their employer. The play perfectly matched Robeson's desire to act in something he believed in—in this case, workers joining together in hopes of getting better treatment. The cast was made up of amateurs—people who had never acted before and spent their daytime hours working

When Pauli attended school in the Soviet Union, he had to write home to keep in touch with his father, Paul Robeson. Above are several stamps of the Soviet Union.

POLITICAL INTERESTS

as carpenters and clerks. Robeson's lead role was originally written for an Irishman and Robeson was excited that the part would now be played by an African American. He did not ask for a salary for his work in *Plant in the Sun*, and he made a point of arriving ahead of time for the evening rehearsals and talking comfortably with the cast. Robeson was a worldwide celebrity and yet his name—along with all the other actors in the play—would be anonymous in the production.

One of the actors, Alfie Bass, said of Robeson, "Nobody I've ever met for intelligence, humanity and so on would ever come up to this man."[6]

The Unity Theatre usually attracted a working-class crowd. But because of Robeson's presence in the show, many wealthy people were also interested in seeing the production. Tickets sold out rapidly for the month's worth of performances and the play was well received by the critics.

Robeson continued keeping himself politically active. He criticized the movie industry throughout the late 1930s. London newspaper columnist Derek Tangye wrote of Robeson: "Here's a man chucking up his career for an ideal which is certain to bring him great unpopularity . . . It showed me that if you feel you have right on your side you can face anything."[7]

Robeson made personal appearances on behalf of many organizations, such as the Spanish Aid Committee, Food

PAUL ROBESON

for Republican Spain Campaign, the Labour and Trade Union Movement, and the Society for Cultural Relations.

He had hoped to travel to Australia in 1939, but the political unrest in Europe made him change his plans. Instead, he went on a concert tour with Lawrence Brown to Norway, Denmark, and Sweden. Often, the masses of people gathered to hear Robeson perform began demonstrating against the Nazis. After Scandinavia, Robeson crossed the Atlantic to spend two months in the United States. He performed in concerts and also spent a week reprising his role in *The Emperor Jones* in White Plains, New York.

Trouble in Europe finally came to a head in September 1939, when Hitler invaded Poland. Only a month earlier, Hitler had signed a pact with Russia, where each country agreed it would not attack the other. Now many people were looking at the Soviet Union with suspicion. Yet Robeson remained firm in his feelings about the Soviet Union.

Many people also were looking at Robeson with suspicion. His outspoken support of the Soviet Union now seemed misplaced. He had been very vocal in supporting labor unions, and he had lent his support to the Republican side in Spain's civil war, a side that was largely made up of Communists. Yet Robeson always stated that his chief interest was in fair treatment for African Americans. He said, "I won't let people forget I'm a

POLITICAL INTERESTS

Robeson got a starring role in the movie *Proud Valley*.

PAUL ROBESON

Negro. If I were Joe Louis, I wouldn't let people forget I'm a Negro either; and if I were Marian Anderson, I would want to be known not as a great singer but as a great Negro singer. It should be the mission of Negro artists to earn respect as Negroes."[8]

Robeson made one more film in England before giving serious thought to returning to the United States. *Proud Valley* told the story of an African-American dockworker who helps coal miners in Wales band together to fight for improved working conditions. The movie would become Robeson's favorite out of all his movies.

He waited until filming was complete before sailing for the United States in late September. Robeson and his wife had spent eleven years in England, but now it was time to go home.

Chapter 8

Under Suspicion

The Robesons took an apartment in Harlem; Pauli and his grandmother lived in the same building. With war raging in Europe, most Americans were in favor of the United States remaining neutral. The mood throughout the country was patriotic and Robeson agreed to perform Earl Robinson's "Ballad for Americans" over the radio.

The broadcast was aired in November 1939 and was a huge success. Not only were hundreds of listeners calling the radio station for two hours after Robeson's performance, but the six hundred people who sat in the studio audience while Robeson was being broadcast, clapped and cheered during the final minutes of the song and continued fifteen minutes after it ended. Robeson also made a

PAUL ROBESON

An American Ballad

"Ballad for Americans" was composed by Earl Robinson, who also happened to be a member of the Communist party. Its original title was "The Ballad for Uncle Sam," and the lyrics touched on the Declaration of Independence, the Revolutionary War, the freeing of the slaves in the American Civil War, and other aspects of American history. It would become a piece that the American people would associate with Robeson.

recording of the song, and it climbed to the top of the charts.

Although Robeson had been chosen by CBS Radio to be the voice of the "Ballad for Americans," he was not allowed to eat in the public dining room of a New York hotel. One of Robeson's friends was visiting from England and—without telling Robeson—invited him to lunch, which was served in her room. Many years later, the friend told Robeson that the hotel told her he could only eat where other hotel guests would not see him.

Robeson played the lead in the Broadway show *John Henry* in January 1940. The part interested him since it was based on the life of a black folk hero. Essie had not thought very highly of the script and did not want her husband to take the part.

UNDER SUSPICION

But Robeson said he wanted "to get back to American folk life. I want to work with my people with whom I belong."[1]

He toured the United States in late winter and spring. Tens of thousands of people gathered to hear him and, as always, they clamored for him to perform the rousing "Ballad for Americans."

In the Hollywood Bowl, more than thirty thousand people sat eagerly to hear Robeson perform. Just days later in Chicago, he sang to more than one hundred sixty thousand people. Although Robeson enjoyed performing and found it rewarding, he always made sure that black and white members of the audience could sit together. He would not perform if the two races were separated.

One Chicago newspaper columnist wrote: "It is easy to understand why Paul Robeson is the most beloved and greatest of artists we have produced. Robeson is an artist-fighter for Negro America . . . He is of the people and for the people."[2]

In the spring of 1941, Robeson bought a home for his family in Enfield, Connecticut. The twelve-room house stood on two and one half acres and included a swimming pool, a billiard room, and a bowling alley, as well as servants' quarters.

On June 22, 1941, Germany betrayed the Soviet Union and invaded it from the west. The Communist country soon joined the main Allied Powers, Britain and the

PAUL ROBESON

United States. Although the Soviet Union was now allied with the United States, Americans still distrusted its Communist government. The Federal Bureau of Investigation began to keep an eye on Robeson. FBI Director J. Edgar Hoover considered Robeson a member of the Communist party, and by 1942, agents kept track of his activities and tapped his telephone. Communists were considered enemies of the United States and its democratic form of government. Robeson, who was a still a strong and outspoken supporter of the Soviet Union, was someone the FBI wanted to keep an eye on.

In 1942, Robeson's last major film, *Tales of Manhattan*, was released. The story—and the cast—had appealed to Robeson at first. The plot revolved around a coat that passed from owner to owner until it was "caught" as it fell from an airplane by a group of sharecroppers in the South. The men eagerly divided up the money in the coat's pockets. Robeson, Ethel Waters, and Eddie Anderson played the sharecroppers. Other names in the movie were Ginger Rogers, Henry Fonda, Rita Hayworth, and Edward G. Robinson.

Robeson had hoped the film would give a realistic portrayal of the lives of poor black sharecroppers. But he was disappointed. When the movie was released, he vowed he was through with Hollywood. From now on, he would make only those movies that reflected his beliefs and

UNDER SUSPICION

portrayed black men and women as respectable human beings, not as children.

With that in mind, Robeson was proud of his work in *Native Land*, a documentary about equal rights that was released in May 1942. Unfortunately, the film came out at a time when the country's mood was patriotic. *Native Land* was considered a Communist film by the FBI. They continued to keep a close watch on Robeson. In spite of this, he continued performing. The role of Othello was one Robeson had played ten years earlier. Although he had been praised for his acting, Robeson wanted to improve how he played the part. He studied the play and worked closely with director Margaret Webster.

Robeson hoped this time he would give an even better performance than when he first played the role. "I am not a great actor like José Ferrer," he said. "All I do is feel the part. I make myself believe I am Othello, and I act as he would act."[3]

When the show opened at the Brattle Theater in Cambridge, Massachusetts, the forty-four-year-old Robeson gave a performance that brought down the house. The audience cheered and applauded and the critics praised Robeson's performance. Although normally the production would have opened on Broadway, this had to wait until October 1943 because Robeson had concerts and political rallies where he had promised to appear.

PAUL ROBESON

This is a scene from Robeson's version of *Othello*. The play was controversial because in it a black man and white woman fall in love.

UNDER SUSPICION

While waiting for *Othello* to open on Broadway, Robeson gave lectures where he discussed his trips to the Soviet Union. He said in that country he found "new life, not death, freedom, not slavery, true human dignity, not inferiority of status."[4]

When the Broadway opening was only six weeks away, Robeson threw himself into his rehearsals. Robeson's work paid off. Opening night on Broadway was even more outstanding than what the actors had experienced in Cambridge. The audience applauded without stopping for twenty minutes.

The show ran on Broadway for ten months and then the production toured the United States and Canada. More than half a million people saw Robeson's performance by the time the show stopped touring. Robeson would never be better known or more popular with the American people.

The impact of the version of *Othello* that Robeson was in was felt in various ways. Awards were heaped on him, including the Page One Award from the New York Newspaper Guild, the Gold Medal from the American Academy of Arts and Sciences for best diction in the American theater, a citation from the national Negro Museum, and the Abraham Lincoln Medal for notable services in human relations.

World War II came to an end in 1945. The Allies—the United States, England, and the Soviet Union—had

PAUL ROBESON

defeated Germany, Japan, and Italy. Although the United States and the Soviet Union had fought on the same side during the war, their different forms of government had created an ever-widening rift between them. The United States was a democracy; the Soviet Union was a Communist country.

Meanwhile, the United States had plenty of trouble of its own. Prejudice against African Americans had been on the rise. Black men were being shot and burned and hanged by angry mobs. It seemed as if law enforcement officers were unable—or unwilling—to stop the lynchings.

To protest the lynchings, Robeson took part in an American Crusade in Washington, D.C., in September 1946. Three thousand delegates—both black and white—came together and Robeson met with President Truman. The meeting, however, did not go well. Truman told Robeson that it was not the right time to pass laws that would stop the lynchings. Robeson replied that if the nation's government would not help protect its black citizens, African Americans would do it on their own.

Two weeks later, Robeson was called to appear before California's Joint Fact-Finding Committee on Un-American Activities. He had to respond to questions for several

> Prejudice against African Americans had been on the rise. Black men were being shot and burned and hanged by angry mobs.

UNDER SUSPICION

hours relating to his possible connection with the Communist party. Senator Jack B. Tenney was head of the committee. When Robeson was asked outright if he was a member of the Communist party, he said that he was not. He also said that he could see himself joining the Communist party "more so today than I could join the Republican or Democratic Party . . . The first people who understood the struggle against fascism and the first to die in it, were Communists."[5]

This would not be the last time Robeson would have to appear before a congressional committee to discuss his beliefs. And as the years went on, Robeson would attract more attention for his beliefs than for his singing or acting.

Chapter 9

In the Thick of It

In the late 1940s, the FBI closely followed Robeson's activities. It seemed as if everywhere he turned, Robeson was asked whether or not he was a Communist. Newspaper reporters hounded him with the question and he always gave the same response: The Communist party was as legal as the Republican or Democratic party and "I could just as well think of joining the Communist Party as any other."[1]

In 1947, Robeson was still a well-liked celebrity who was able to draw crowds to his concerts. He was included in the list of runners-up when Americans were asked to name their ten favorite people. He was still performing to enormous crowds in Boston and New York City.

Many of his concerts were on behalf of the political groups he supported, such as the Civil Rights Congress

IN THE THICK OF IT

A Progressive Candidate

Henry Wallace had served as President Truman's secretary of commerce. He was asked to resign from the post because he disapproved of Truman's hard line against the Soviet Union. Wallace believed that although the United States and the Soviet Union had different forms of government and economic systems, they could still cooperate and enjoy a peaceful coexistence. But Truman's policy toward the Soviet Union was not a flexible one; Wallace was asked to leave.

Robeson, not surprisingly, agreed with Wallace and the Progressive party. Not only did Progressives stand for improving U.S. relations with the Soviet Union, the party also focused on equal rights for all American citizens as its goal.

PAUL ROBESON

and the Joint Anti-Fascist Refugee Committee. With an election year looming ahead, the Progressive party was trying to gain a foothold. The party's candidate for president was Henry A. Wallace, former secretary of agriculture and vice president under Franklin D. Roosevelt.

Wallace's candidacy for president was officially announced in December 1947. One of the names suggested as his vice presidential running mate was Paul Robeson. Yet Robeson chose not to run for vice president. Instead, he worked toward getting the Progressive candidate elected. Wallace had a lot of support from black voters at the start of the campaign. But Truman cut into this by ordering that blacks and whites serve together in the armed forces. Truman also gave a speech on civil rights in Harlem.

Robeson spent much of his time campaigning for Wallace in the southern states. This was a courageous act since the color of Robeson's skin made him an obvious target. Also, he was speaking on behalf of a political party that had little support among southerners.

Whenever Robeson spoke, members of the Progressive party gathered tightly around him, physically protecting him from the possible violence that could erupt at any moment. Robeson met men whose lives had been threatened by the Ku Klux Klan—a racist group known for its violent activities—simply for supporting the Progressive party. He met an African-American newspaper

IN THE THICK OF IT

editor who had watched the Klan erect a burning cross on his lawn.

"They won't run me out," the editor, Lark Marshall of the Macon *World*, said to Robeson. "They might carry me out, but they'll never run me out."[2]

Robeson took heart at the courage he saw throughout the South. While Robeson worked hard campaigning for Wallace, the FBI continued following him and keeping track of his activities. Although they were unable to gather information that directly linked Robeson with the Communist party, they continued to build up a file against him.

For all Robeson's efforts to promote the Progressive party in the presidential election, Wallace lost by a large amount. He received little more than 1 million votes, while Truman received 24 million and Dewey pulled in close to 22 million.

In the spring of 1949, Robeson attended the World Peace Congress in Paris, France. Fifty countries sent a combined total of two thousand delegates to the conference. When Robeson stood before the Congress, he gave a speech that created a huge uproar in the United States. He said that African Americans should not consider fighting in a war against the Soviet Union.

"Our will to fight for peace is strong. We shall not make war on anyone," he said in his April 20 speech.[3]

However, when the Associated Press news service quoted Robeson's speech, the words were changed.

PAUL ROBESON

According to the story that ran in the newspapers, Robeson said, "It is unthinkable . . . that American Negroes would go to war on behalf of those who have oppressed us for generations . . . against a country [the Soviet Union] which in one generation has raised our people to the full dignity of manhood."[4]

This is not what Robeson said, but this is the story that appeared in the newspapers. Not only was Robeson apparently saying that black Americans should not fight on behalf of the United States, he was stating that the Soviet way of life was better than the American way.

Immediately, Robeson was called a traitor to his country by journalists and political figures across the United States. Even leaders of the black community turned against Robeson, saying he was giving his own personal opinion and not speaking for blacks in general. The leaders of black organizations made it clear that they were loyal to the United States—not to Robeson. In their eyes—and the eyes of most of white

◆◆◆◆◆
This button captures how Paul Robeson could inspire the people around him.

94

IN THE THICK OF IT

America—not only had Robeson spoken out against the United States in favor of its enemy, the Soviet Union, but he had made this speech while he was in another country. If Robeson had criticized America while he was actually in the United States, the reaction to the speech would probably not have been as severe.

Robeson tried to tell journalists that his words had not been quoted accurately. Several weeks after the speech, an accurate version of his statement was printed in several black newspapers. Yet none of the country's major newspapers ran the corrected speech. Robeson continued to protest that his speech emphasized the fight for peace, not people going to war against another country.

But the damage had been done. For many Americans—black and white—Paul Robeson had become an enemy of the United States. With little chance of performing in the United States, Robeson headed to England where he gave a concert tour. He said he wanted to "make it perfectly clear that the world is wide, and a few pressures (will) not stop my career."[5]

Robeson continued traveling throughout Europe and the Soviet Union singing to large crowds. In Moscow, Robeson was concerned that he could not find many of his Jewish friends. He eventually learned of the arrests and, in many cases, deaths of several friends at the hands of the Soviet Union's secret police. Still, Robeson would not speak out against the Soviet Union. Through the remaining

PAUL ROBESON

years of his life, Robeson would not criticize the country he had idealized for so long.

When Robeson returned to the United States in June, he had little time to worry about the reaction to his speech. His son Pauli—Paul, Jr., now—was getting married in three days to Marilyn Paula Greenberg, a white Jewish woman whom he had met at Cornell University. The couple was married in a private ceremony in the minister's own apartment. Yet as soon as the wedding party left the building, they faced an angry crowd of hundreds of people who were screaming at them. They also received hate mail in days to come.

Robeson was furious about the reaction to his son's marriage. He went that same day to a rally put on by the Council on African Affairs in Harlem. The crowd consisted of forty-five hundred people—an equal mix of black and white—and the rally lasted nearly five hours.

"I am born and bred in this America of ours," Robeson told the crowd. "I want to love it . . . But it's up to the rest of America when I shall love it with the same intensity that I love the Negro people . . ."[6]

He also said blacks should not fight in battles unless they were fighting for equal rights in their own country.

Newspaper headlines the next day blasted Robeson for his speech. The papers claimed he loved the Soviet Union better than the United States; they said he was not a welcome citizen in his own country.

IN THE THICK OF IT

The House Un-American Activities Committee held hearings in July to hear statements from African Americans about Robeson's remarks that blacks should not fight on behalf of their country. Many famous African Americans testified, including Jackie Robinson, the first African-American baseball player to play in the major leagues in modern times. Robinson said that the charges by Robeson of unfair treatment against blacks in the United States were accurate and it did not matter whether these remarks were made by a Communist or anyone else. However, Robinson went on to say that "we can win our fight without the Communists and we don't want their help." He said Robeson's urging of blacks not to fight against the Soviet Union was "silly."[7]

Jackie Robinson was praised by the newspapers and politicians for his comments, while Robeson fell even lower in the public's opinion. But Robeson was a determined man, and in August 1949 he decided to travel to Peekskill, New York, to give a concert on behalf of Harlem's Civil Rights Congress.

Even as Robeson boarded a train in New York City, he was aware that there might be trouble at the concert. Various organizations, such as the Veterans of Foreign Wars and the American Legion, were angry at Robeson's turning his back on the United States and his support of America's enemy, Russia. They were threatening to make

PAUL ROBESON

Rioters at Robeson's concert in Peekskill pose in front of a wrecked car.

IN THE THICK OF IT

trouble if he appeared in Peekskill. And there was trouble, right from the start.

Protestors were already gathering and a truck blocked the middle of the road, bringing the concert traffic to a virtual standstill. Crowds of people yelled insults, such as "Dirty Commie," and hurled rocks at the cars. On one hill stood a burning cross. There were police in the area, but they did not try to stop the protestors.

Robeson was furious about what was happening and was ready to get out of his car and confront the angry mob. But friends convinced him it would be too dangerous and he was driven away from the area. Meanwhile, the crowd moved onto the concert grounds. They destroyed the stage, set fire to the chairs for the audience, and attacked the people who had planned on attending the concert. Twelve concertgoers had to be taken to the hospital.

Writer Howard Fast said, "They [more than five hundred protestors] had worked themselves into a screaming alcoholic frenzy and they repeated their threats that no one would leave the picnic grounds alive . . . they tore up the fence rails and used them as weapons."[8]

Three days after the riot, more than three thousand people gathered at the Golden Gate Ballroom in Harlem to protest what had happened in Peekskill. Robeson sang and gave a speech about not giving in to more violence.

PAUL ROBESON

"We'll have our meetings and our concerts all over these United States," he told the crowd. "And we'll see that our women and our children are not harmed again!"[9]

Robeson decided to return to Peekskill to try and give the concert. It was to be held on September 4 about a mile from where the first concert should have taken place. More than two thousand volunteers showed up to keep the concertgoers safe—yet those protesting Robeson's appearance numbered eight thousand. The protestors threatened that the audience might enter the concert grounds, but they would not be allowed to leave.

Robeson took the stage around four o'clock, after performances by Pete Seeger, Ray Lev, and Leonid Hambro. Larry Brown accompanied Robeson on piano as he sang "Let My People Go" and "Ol' Man River."

Security men spotted several protestors with guns hiding in the surrounding area. But Robeson stood his ground. When he finished his performance, he was led to a car where the windows were covered with blankets. Robeson lay down on the floor in the back of the car; two bodyguards protected him by covering Robeson with their own bodies.

As the concertgoers headed home, violence erupted. Many policemen at the scene joined the

IN THE THICK OF IT

protestors as people were clubbed, beaten, and dragged through the dirt. Rocks and glass flew through the air; thousands of car windows were smashed. More than one hundred people were injured.

New York's governor, Thomas E. Dewey, called for an investigation. But the report concluded that neither the protestors nor the police had done anything wrong.

Robeson vowed to continue giving concerts and to continue delivering his message throughout the country. "I refuse to let my personal success . . . explain away the injustices to fourteen million of my people," he said, "because with all the energy at my command, I fight for the right of the Negro people and other oppressed labor-driven Americans to have decent homes, decent jobs, and the dignity that belongs to every human being!"[10]

Chapter 10

A Career Halted

Robeson continued to travel and give concerts. He expected there to be problems—and there were. When he planned to visit Pittsburgh, Pennsylvania; Akron, Ohio; and Cincinnati, Ohio, he met with resistance. Local officials banded together to prevent Robeson from using their facilities for holding concerts. When Robeson was told he would have to take the stage at Oberlin College with an African-American minister who was against Robeson's beliefs, Robeson decided not to travel to the Ohio college.

Still, there were occasions—such as appearances in Chicago—where Robeson was able to speak and the turnout was strong. Yet when Robeson was slated to appear in Los Angeles, the city council passed a resolution telling citizens not to attend the concert. Meanwhile the

A CAREER HALTED

NAACP Youth Council in Los Angeles urged young people—of all races—to support Robeson and appear at the concert. In the end, fifteen thousand people attended the concert. There was no outbreak of violence, although several African-American policemen stayed near Robeson just in case.

At an appearance in Washington, D.C., police ringed the arena for six blocks around the area where Robeson was to speak.

Robeson tried to continue traveling and lecturing, but it was becoming more and more difficult. He was scheduled to appear on Eleanor Roosevelt's television show *Today With Mrs. Roosevelt*. But a day later, it was announced by an NBC spokesperson that Robeson would not be on the show.

In May 1950, Robeson headed to London to attend the World Peace Council. The conference drew twenty thousand people and although there were many speakers, no one received louder applause than Robeson. He performed songs of America, China, and the Soviet Union.

One month after the peace conference, the North Koreans invaded South Korea. Robeson said, "I have said it before and say it again, that the place for the Negro people to fight for their freedom is here at home."[1]

Planning to travel to Europe that summer, the fifty-two-year-old Robeson was told he could not leave the country. The State Department took away his passport.

They did not give a specific reason why Robeson could not leave the United States, merely that it would not be in the country's best interests.

There were a few demonstrations on Robeson's behalf, the largest in Harlem when a crowd of six thousand turned out to protest the removal of his passport. But generally, the country was quiet. Robeson, who so recently had been considered one of the most popular Americans, was no longer beloved by the majority of people. They felt he had been too outspoken for too long in his praise of a country that was considered America's enemy. And now with the onset of the Korean War, patriotism was climbing again; Robeson's support of the Soviet Union was not appreciated.

Robeson made two different attempts to fight what was happening to him. First, he worked with W.E.B. Du Bois, a black civil-rights activist, to put out a publication called *Freedom*. In December 1950, the first issue of the monthly journal appeared. Robeson wrote an article explaining his actions and beliefs. Hoover and the FBI considered *Freedom* a Communist publication.

"I am simply fulfilling my obligation—my responsibility, as best as I can and know, to the human family to which I proudly belong," Robeson wrote.[2] *Freedom* lasted five years before folding.

Meanwhile, Robeson's lawyers were working to get his passport back. The lawyers claimed that Robeson's constitutional rights—such as freedom of speech and freedom of

A CAREER HALTED

> ### African-American Criticism
> Times were difficult for Robeson. When the celebrated African-American boxer Sugar Ray Robinson returned to the United States early in 1951 after a tour of Europe, he accused Robeson of spreading Communist propaganda. Dodgers baseball player Don Newcombe almost wound up in a fight with Robeson. The black pitcher told Robeson in a Harlem restaurant, "I'm joining the Army to fight people like you."[3] Robeson became angry, and people standing nearby had to separate the two men before the argument grew physical.

thought—were being denied him. They also said that he was unable to earn a living if he could not travel out of the country. Yet after five months, the case was dismissed and Robeson was still not allowed to leave the United States.

Later that year, Robeson's name was left off the list of people who had won the NAACP's Springarn Medal. Although Robeson had been honored with the award in 1945, the *Amsterdam News* did not include his name on their list.

Robeson received yet another blow when the State Department would not allow him to perform at a concert in Vancouver, British Columbia, in 1952. Although Robeson did not need a passport to travel to Canada, he was told that during a national emergency, the government

PAUL ROBESON

could prevent a citizen from leaving the country. Robeson stayed in Seattle, Washington, and sang to the United Mine, Mill, and Smelter Workers Union over a telephone that was hooked up to a loudspeaker in Vancouver.

When Robeson performed at the Peace Arch Park on the U.S.-Canadian border, he looked out on a crowd of forty thousand and told them:

> I stand here today under great stress because I dared, as do all of you, to fight for peace and a decent life for all men, women and children wherever they may be. And especially today I stand fighting for the rights of my people in this America in which I was born . . . I am the same Paul, fighting a little harder because the times call for harder struggle.[4]

Robeson was awarded the 1952 International Stalin Peace Prize by the Soviet Union that came attached with $25,000. He was the only American of the seven recipients to receive the award, which honored people from any country who gave their service to help stop war. Robeson once again tried to get back his passport so he could claim the prize, but the United States government would not let him.

Robeson's politics were making his life difficult, and it affected his son as well. Paul, Jr., had graduated in engineering in the top 10 percent of his class at Cornell University. Yet he could not get hired anywhere because of his last name. At one point, he was about to get a job in a physics lab, but the FBI intervened and prevented Paul from being hired.

A CAREER HALTED

Robeson was a fierce protector of civil rights for African Americans.

PAUL ROBESON

Robeson's hands were tied. He could not give concerts abroad because he had no passport, and his audience was growing smaller and smaller in his own country. He was forced into turning down opportunities to perform *Othello* and give concerts overseas. He was invited to appear at peace conferences. Yet without a passport, he had to refuse. In the United States, the Brooklyn Academy of Music would not hold a cultural festival when Robeson declared he would perform there.

Robeson now began to suffer periods of depression. His friend Louise Patterson, said, "To a man with his tremendous energy and creativity, it was a terrible period. [It was] worse . . . than being in prison . . . He was in a little room and he would sit up there with his records."[5]

He spent some time living with his brother Benjamin, a pastor of the Mother A.M.E. Zion Church in Harlem. Robeson tried and failed again in 1955 to get back his passport. It came to nothing when he again refused to sign a form stating whether or not he belonged to the Communist party.

Robeson had to have surgery toward the end of the year. Recovering from the operation and suffering from depression had caused him to lose weight. Although at times he felt confused and exhausted, Robeson sometimes felt energetic and would spend hours studying music theory.

A CAREER HALTED

In the midst of this severe depression in July 1956, Robeson was ordered to appear before the House Committee on Un-American Activities. Family and friends worried that Robeson was mentally too weak to handle the hearing. Yet he rose to the occasion.

Time and again, he was asked whether he was a member of the Communist party. And time and again, Robeson avoided the question. He laughed when committee members asked him if his Communist party name was "John Thomas."

"My name is Paul Robeson, and anything I have to say or stand for I have said in public all over the world—and that is why I am here today," he said.[6] When Robeson was asked about the Soviet Union, he said he was interested in the United States, and that the Soviet Union's problems were its own.

Robeson's strong appearance before the committee lifted him briefly out of his depression. He traveled to New Jersey where he met with several African-American groups. By the summer of 1957, the State Department agreed that he could travel to such places as Alaska, Hawaii, and Puerto Rico where a passport was not needed.

Supporters of Robeson's in England joined together to form the National Paul Robeson Committee, where they worked to have his passport returned. Members of this group included twenty-seven members of England's Parliament. The British Actors Equity also worked on

PAUL ROBESON

Robeson's behalf when they voted to try and help Robeson so he could perform once again in England.

Robeson began giving concerts throughout the United States, and in 1958 he came out with his autobiography, *Here I Stand*. The book focused on Robeson's loyalty to African Americans and not on his political views. While white journalists ignored the autobiography, the black newspapers not only reviewed the book but praised Robeson's courage.

Vanguard Records brought Robeson back into the studio and everyone there was amazed at how strong Robeson's voice sounded. Soon after this, Actors' Equity in the United States voted to ask the State Department to return Robeson's passport.

When Robeson turned sixty in 1958, his birthday was celebrated in more than twenty-five countries, including China, the Soviet Union, East and West Germany, and many African nations. He performed to a full house at Carnegie Hall a month later, and although his voice did not have the depth and richness of previous years, the sheer power of his personality was as strong as ever.

Finally, in June 1958, the Supreme Court ruled that the State Department did not have the right to take away the passport of an American citizen because of his beliefs. The vote was five to four, and it was exactly what Robeson had been arguing from the start. After eight years, Robeson could once again travel. He immediately

A CAREER HALTED

made plans to travel to London and perform in *Othello* for the Stratford-on-Avon theater's hundredth anniversary.

"It will be good to hear applause again," he said.[7]

More than two hundred British men and women cheered Robeson when his plane landed in England in July 1958. The following month, Robeson and Essie flew to Moscow where they were given a grand reception and met with Soviet officials. However, in Moscow Robeson became sick; he suffered from exhaustion. Once a large man, Robeson was now thin and looked weak; he wore heavy glasses. But he was determined to play Othello at Stratford-on-Avon. When he performed the role in April 1959, it would be the last time he appeared on stage in a play. The show was well reviewed and ran seven months. Robeson was only well enough to appear twice a week.

At age sixty-two, Robeson began making up for the years he had lost when he did not have a passport. He traveled again to the Soviet Union and also put on concerts in Wales, East Germany, Australia, and New Zealand.

Although Robeson continued making plans for more concerts and even a possible film version of *Othello*, he was not up to the challenge of travel—physically or mentally.

> When Robeson turned sixty in 1958, his birthday was celebrated in more than twenty-five countries.

PAUL ROBESON

Robeson's most famous performance was in *Othello*.

A CAREER HALTED

He had frequent dizzy spells and had problems with his circulatory system. Suffering again from depression, Robeson tried to take his own life in March 1961 when he was in Moscow.

After being hospitalized in Moscow, he now shuttled back and forth between the Soviet Union and England. His depression was severe and he was given shock treatments and high doses of drugs.

In the winter of 1963, Robeson decided to return to the United States. Occasionally he appeared in public to make a speech concerning civil rights.

In December 1965, Essie died and Robeson was cared for by his son Paul, Jr., and his sister, Marian. Their marriage had lasted more than forty years and Essie's death was a devastating blow to Robeson.

In 1967, he sang in public—for the first time in four years—at a party held by *Freedomways* magazine.

The last years of Robeson's life were quiet. He was honored when Rutgers University opened the Paul Robeson Campus Center in 1972. The following year a tribute to him was held at Carnegie Hall for his seventy-fifth birthday. Performers included Pete Seeger, Sidney Poitier, James Earl Jones, and Harry Belafonte.

"Here at home, my heart is with the continuing struggle . . . to gain for all black Americans and the other minority groups not only equal rights but an equal share," said Robeson.[8]

PAUL ROBESON

Paul Robeson, Jr., poses with a stamp honoring his father.

A CAREER HALTED

By the time Robeson turned seventy-five, he was able to look back proudly on what he had tried to accomplish. "People should understand that when I could be active I went here and there and everywhere," he said. "What I wanted to do I did; what I wanted to say I said, and now that ill health has compelled my retirement I have decided to let the record speak for itself. As far as my basic outlook is concerned, everybody should know that I'm the same Paul Robeson . . ."[9]

Honors continued to come to Robeson, such as an award established in his name by the AFL-CIO, a workers' union. He was also awarded an honorary Doctor of Law degree by his father's college, Lincoln University. Yet Robeson was too sickly to enjoy these honors. In December 1975, he suffered a small stroke and entered a Philadelphia hospital. He died several weeks later on January 23, 1976, at the age of seventy-seven.

Paul Robeson devoted his life to becoming the best he could be—whether it was at sports, in school, or working toward equal rights for all Americans. He was a passionate man who gave his life to his beliefs.

Chronology

1898—Born April 9 in Princeton, New Jersey.

1904—Paul's mother, Maria, dies of burns when her dress catches fire.

1915—Attends Rutgers College.

1919—Moves to New York City and attends law school.

1920—Appears in his first play, *Simon the Cyrenian*.

1923—Works at a New York law firm.

1924—Performs in *The Emperor Jones* and *All God's Chillun Got Wings*.

1925—Begins performing spirituals with Lawrence Brown.

1928—Performs in *Show Boat* in London.

1930—Performs in *Othello*.

1934—Makes first visit to Soviet Union.

1935—Stars in film version of *The Emperor Jones*.

1945—Receives the Springarn Medal, the NAACP's highest honor.

1948—Gives concert in Peekskill, New York where violence erupts.

1950—Passport is taken away.

1952—Wins Stalin Peace Prize.

1958—Publishes autobiography, *Here I Stand*.

CHRONOLOGY

1959—Stars in seven-month run of *Othello* in England.

1965—Makes last official public appearance.

1972—Receives the Ira Aldridge Award for lifetime achievement from the Association for the Study of African American Life and History.

1976—Dies January 23 in Philadelphia at age 77.

Chapter Notes

Chapter 1. Rising to the Top

1. Dorothy Butler Gilliam, *Paul Robeson: All-American* (Washington, D.C.: The New Republic Book Company, Inc., 1976), p. 16.

Chapter 2. Years of Hardship

1. Eslanda Goode Robeson, *Paul Robeson, Negro* (New York: Harper & Brothers, 1930), p. 161.

2. Dorothy Butler Gilliam, *Paul Robeson: All-American* (Washington, D.C.: The New Republic Book Company, Inc., 1976), p. 9.

3. Martin Duberman, *Paul Robeson* (New York: Knopf, 1988), p. 9.

4. Paul Robeson, *Here I Stand* (Boston: Beacon Press, 1958), p. 16.

5. Ibid., p. 9.

6. Ibid.

7. Paul Robeson, Jr., *The Undiscovered Paul Robeson: An Artist's Journey, 1898–1939* (New York: John Wiley & Sons, Inc.), p. 14.

8. Duberman, pp. 14–15.

9. Ibid., p. 17.

CHAPTER NOTES

10. Paul Robeson, *Here I Stand*, p. 25.

Chapter 3. College and Career Choices

1. Martin Duberman, *Paul Robeson* (New York: Knopf, 1988), p. 23.

2. Ibid., p. 27.

3. Dorothy Butler Gilliam, *Paul Robeson: All-American* (Washington, D.C.: The New Republic Book Company, Inc., 1976), p. 26.

4. Paul Robeson, Jr., *The Undiscovered Paul Robeson: An Artist's Journey, 1898–1939* (New York: John Wiley & Sons, Inc.), p. 56.

5. Ibid., p. 57.

Chapter 4. On Stage

1. Martin Duberman, *Paul Robeson* (New York: Knopf, 1988), p. 55.

2. Ibid., p. 59.

3. Ibid.

4. Ibid., p. 63.

5. Philip S. Foner, ed., *Paul Robeson Speaks: Writings, Speeches, Interviews, 1918–1974* (New York: Brunner/Mazel Publishers, 1978), p. 68.

6. Paul Robeson, Jr., *The Undiscovered Paul Robeson: An Artist's Journey, 1898–1939* (New York: John Wiley & Sons, Inc.), p. 87.

7. Foner, p. 69.

8. Paul Robeson, *Here I Stand* (Boston: Beacon Press, 1958), p. 49.

9. Paul Robeson, Jr., p. 94.

10. Marie Seton, *Paul Robeson*. (London: Dennis Dobson, 1958), p. 40.

11. Duberman, p. 98.

Chapter 5. Beyond the United States

1. Martin Duberman, *Paul Robeson* (New York: Knopf, 1988), p. 105.

2. Paul Robeson, Jr., *The Undiscovered Paul Robeson: An Artist's Journey, 1898–1939* (New York: John Wiley & Sons, Inc.), p. 141.

3. Sheila Tully Boyle and Andrew Bunie, *Paul Robeson: The Years of Promise and Achievement* (Amherst: University of Massachusetts Press, 2001), p. 192.

4. Dorothy Butler Gilliam, *Paul Robeson: All-American* (Washington, D.C.: The New Republic Book Company, Inc., 1976), p. 60.

Chapter 6. The Spell of the Soviet Union

1. Martin Duberman, *Paul Robeson* (New York: Knopf, 1988), p. 156.

2. Paul Robeson, Jr., *The Undiscovered Paul Robeson: An Artist's Journey, 1898–1939* (New York: John Wiley & Sons, Inc.), p. 194.

3. Ibid., p. 198.

4. Ibid., p. 185.

5. Duberman, p. 175.

CHAPTER NOTES

6. Dorothy Butler Gilliam, *Paul Robeson: All-American* (Washington, D.C.: The New Republic Book Company, Inc., 1976), pp. 82–83.

7. Ibid., p. 83.

8. Gilliam, p. 80.

9. Philip S. Foner, ed., *Paul Robeson Speaks: Writings, Speeches, Interviews, 1918–1974* (New York: Brunner/Mazel Publishers, 1978), p. 91.

10. Duberman, p. 204.

Chapter 7. Political Interests

1. Paul Robeson, Jr., *The Undiscovered Paul Robeson: An Artist's Journey, 1898–1939* (New York: John Wiley & Sons, Inc.), p. 242.

2. Martin Duberman, *Paul Robeson* (New York: Knopf, 1988), p. 209.

3. Ibid., p. 210.

4. Ibid., p. 220.

5. Ibid.

6. Ibid., p. 224.

7. Paul Robeson, Jr., p. 315.

8. Ibid., p. 325.

Chapter 8. Under Suspicion

1. Sheila Tully Boyle and Andrew Bunie, *Paul Robeson: The Years of Promise and Achievement* (Amherst: University of Massachusetts Press, 2001), p. 421.

2. Dorothy Butler Gilliam, *Paul Robeson: All-American* (Washington, D.C.: The New Republic Book Company, Inc., 1976), p. 101.

3. Ibid., p. 108.

4. Ibid., p. 113.

5. Martin Duberman, *Paul Robeson* (New York: Knopf, 1988), p. 308.

Chapter 9. In the Thick of It

1. Martin Duberman, *Paul Robeson* (New York: Knopf, 1988), p. 318.

2. Ibid., p. 327.

3. Ibid., p. 342.

4. Dorothy Butler Gilliam, *Paul Robeson: All-American* (Washington, D.C.: The New Republic Book Company, Inc., 1976), p. 137.

5. Ibid.

6. Duberman, p. 358.

7. Ibid., p. 360.

8. Gilliam, p. 150.

9. Duberman, p. 367.

10. Philip S. Foner, ed., *Paul Robeson Speaks: Writings, Speeches, Interviews, 1918–1974* (New York: Brunner/Mazel Publishers, 1978), p. 260.

Chapter 10. A Career Halted

1. Martin Duberman, *Paul Robeson* (New York: Knopf, 1988), p. 388.

2. Ibid., p. 393.

CHAPTER NOTES

3. Ibid. p. 396.

4. Dorothy Butler Gilliam, *Paul Robeson: All-American* (Washington, D.C.: The New Republic Book Company, Inc., 1976), p. 163.

5. Ibid., p. 162.

6. Duberman, p. 440.

7. Ibid., p. 463.

8. Ibid., p. 482.

9. Gilliam, p. 186.

Further Reading

Bolden, Tonya. *Portraits of African-American Heroes.* New York: Dutton Children's Books, 2003.

———. *Tell All the Children Our Story: Memories and Momentoes of Being Young and Black in America.* New York: Harry N. Abrams, 2001.

Carrick Hill, Laban. *Harlem Stomp!: A Cultural History of the Harlem Renaissance.* New York: Little, Brown, 2003.

Haskins, Jim. *Black Stars of the Civil Rights Movement.* Hoboken, N.J.: John Wiley & Sons, 2003.

Healy, Nick. *Paul Robeson.* Chicago: Raintree, 2003.

Katz, William Loren. *Black Legacy: A History of New York's African Americans.* New York: Atheneum Books for Young Readers, 1997.

Seidman, David. *Civil Rights.* New York: Rosen Pub. Group, 2001.

Internet Addresses

American Masters: Paul Robeson
<http://www.pbs.org/wnet/americanmasters/database/robeson_p.html>

Paul Robeson: Artist and Citizen
<http://www.npg.si.edu/exh/robeson/robes2.htm>

Rutgers Paul Robeson Web Site
<http://www.scc.rutgers.edu/njh/PaulRobeson/>

Index

Page numbers for photographs are in **boldface** type.

A
Abraham Lincoln Medal, 87
Ackerman, Dr., 18, 19, 21
Akron Pros, 28, 29
All God's Chillun Got Wings, 37, 38, 39, **40**, 41, 43, 61

B
Big Fella, 71
Black Boy, 50
Body and Soul, 43
Borderline, 54
Brown, Lawrence, **42**, 43, 44, 47, 48, 50, 51, 52, 71, 78
Bustill, Maria Louisa (mother), 10, 12, 13–14

C
Cap and Skull Honor Society, 26
Carnegie Hall, 54, 110, 113
Castillo, Fernando, 75
Civil Rights Congress, 90, 97
Civil War, 12, 38, 82
Columbia University Law School, 27–28, 29, 31
Coppicus, F. C., 53–54
Counsel on African Affairs in Harlem, 96

D
Dewey, Thomas E., 101
Downer Street St. Luke A.M.E. Zion Church, 15, 16
Du Bois, W.E.B., 104

E
The Emperor Jones, 39, 43, 44, 45, **46**, 47, 50, 56, 61, 78

F
Fast, Howard, 99
Federal Bureau of Investigation (FBI), 84, 85, 90, 93, 104, 106
Food for Republican Spain Campaign, 77–78
The Four Harmony Kings, 33
Fourteenth Amendment, 26

G
Georgia Tech, 22
Goldman, Emma, 58
Goode, Eslanda (Essie), 28, 29, **30**, 31, 32, 34, 39, 44, 45, 47, 48, 50, 51, 52, 54, 57, 65, 68, 71, 73, 75, 82, 111, 113
Grand Central Station, 25
Green Bay, Wisconsin, 48
Greenberg, Marilyn Paula, 96
Greenwich, Conn., 31

H
The Hairy Ape, 57
Hamlet, 19
Harlem Renaissance, 75
Harlem, New York, 28, 32, 81, 92, 99, 104, 105, 108
Harlem's Civil Rights Congress, 97

126

INDEX

Hemingway, Ernest, 47
Here I Stand, 110
Hitler, Adolf, 64, 78
Hollywood Bowl, 83
Hollywood, California, 68, 84
Hoover, J. Edgar, 84, 104
House Un-American Activities Committee, 97, 109
Hughes, Langston, 47
Hylan, James, 41

I

International Stalin Peace Prize, 106

J

James J. Jamison School, 17–18
Jericho, 71, 73
John Henry, 82
Joint Anti-Fascist Refugee Committee, 92
Joyce, James, 47

K

King Solomon's Mines, 69, 70, 72
Korda, Zoltan, 62

L

Labour and Trade Union Movement, 77
Light, Jimmy, 56, 57
Lincoln University, 12, 28, 115
L'Ouverture, Toussaint, 21, 64, 67, 68

M

Macgowan, Kenneth, 37
The Magic Flute, 73
McKay, Claude, 71
Metropolitan Music Bureau, 54

Milwaukee Badgers, 28

N

National Association for the Advancement of Colored People (NAACP), 103, 105
National Paul Robeson Committee, 109
Native Land, 85
Neale, Geraldine Maimie, 27, 31
Negro Museum, 87
New York Newspaper Guild, 87

O

O'Neill, Eugene, 37, 57
Othello, 19, 54, 56, 57, 85, **86**, 87, 108, 111, **112**
Orchestra Hall, 48

P

Page One Award, 87
Paul Robeson Campus Center, 113
Paul Robeson, Negro, 57
Phi Beta Kappa, 27
Phillipsburg High School, 19
Plant in the Sun, 75, 76, 77
Plantation Revue, 35
Porgy, 51
Princeton, New Jersey, 10, 12, 13
Proud Valley, **79**, 80
Provincetown Players, 37, 41, 43, 56
Provincetown Playhouse, 37
Pygmalion, 52

R

Robeson, Paul Leroy, **6, 26, 30, 49, 53, 55, 65, 76, 107**

as athlete, 7–9, 19, **20**, 22, **23**, 24, 28, 29, 31
birth, 10
college, 22–27
death, 115
high school, 18–21
marriage, 31
political activism, 62, 67, 73–75, 78, 83, 84–85, 86, 88–89, 90, 92–97, 99–101, 103–106, 109
siblings, 10, 14
Robeson, Paul, Jr. (Pauli), 51, 59, 61, 65, **66**, 70, 71, 73, 75, 81, 96, 106, 113, **114**
Robeson, William Drew (father), 10, 12, 13, 14, 15, 16, 17, 25, 27
Robinson, Earl, 81, 82
Romeo and Juliet, 19
Roseanne, 38
Rutgers College, 7, 8, 21, 22–24, 26, 27, 35, 59, 113

S

Sanders of the River, 62
Sanford, G. Foster, 9, 35
Sarron, Bernard, 52
Seton, Marie, 65
Shakespeare at the Water Cure, 19
Show Boat, 51, 52, 59, **60**, 67–68
Shuffle Along, 33
Simon the Cyrenian, 32
Society for Cultural Relations, 77
Somerville High School, 18
Somerville, New Jersey, 16, 17, 18
Song of Freedom, 68–**69**
Spanish Aid Committee, 77
Spanish Civil War, 74
St. Thomas A.M.E. Zion Church, 16
Stein, Gertrude, 47
Stotesbury, Louis William, 35

T

Taboo, 32, 33
Tales of Manhattan, 84
Tangye, Derek, 77
The Time Machine, 52

U

Underground Railroad, 10, 12
Union Army, 12
Unity Theatre, 75, 77

V

Van Volkenburg, Nellie, 56
Vanguard Records, 110
Victor Company, 47

W

Wallace, Henry A., 91, 92, 93
The War of the Worlds, 52
Washington and Lee University, 22
The Washington School, 18
Webster, Margaret, 85
Wells, H. G., 52
West Virginia University, 23, 24
Westfield, New Jersey, 14, 16
Wilborg, Mary Hoyt, 33
Wilcoxon, Henry, 73
William and Mary College, 22
Witherspoon Street Presbyterian Church, 12
World Peace Council, 103

B R653F HHEIX
Ford, Carin T.
Paul Robeson : I want to make freedom ring /
HEIGHTS
07/12